BY DEBORAH ELLIS

Fiction
Looking for X
The Breadwinner
Parvana's Journey
Mud City
The Breadwinner Trilogy
A Company of Fools
The Heaven Shop
I Am a Taxi
Sacred Leaf
Jackal in the Garden: An Encounter with Bihzad
Jakeman
Bifocal (*co-written with Eric Walters*)
Lunch with Lenin and Other Stories
No Safe Place
True Blue
No Ordinary Day

Nonfiction
Three Wishes: Israeli and Palestinian Children Speak
Our Stories, Our Songs: African Children Talk about AIDS
Off to War: Voices of Soldiers' Children
Children of War: Voices of Iraqi Refugees
Kids of Kabul: Living Bravely through a Never-ending War
Looks Like Daylight: Voices of Indigenous Kids

MY NAME IS PARVANA

MY NAME IS PARVANA

DEBORAH ELLIS

GROUNDWOOD BOOKS
HOUSE OF ANANSI PRESS
TORONTO   BERKELEY

Groundwood Books / House of Anansi Press
110 Spadina Avenue, Suite 801
Toronto, Ontario M5V 2K4
or c/o Publishers Group West
1700 Fourth Street, Berkeley, CA 94710

"Resume," from *Dorothy Parker: Complete Poems* by Dorothy Parker, copyright
© 1999 by The National Association for the Advancement of Colored People.
Used by permission of Penguin, a division of Penguin Group (USA) Inc.

We acknowledge for their financial support of our publishing program the Canada
Council for the Arts, the Government of Canada through the Canada Book Fund
(CBF) and the Ontario Arts Council.

**Canada Council
for the Arts**   **Conseil des Arts
du Canada**

**ONTARIO ARTS COUNCIL
CONSEIL DES ARTS DE L'ONTARIO**

Library and Archives Canada Cataloguing in Publication
Ellis, Deborah
My name is Parvana / Deborah Ellis.
Issued also in an electronic format.
ISBN 978-1-55498-297-4
I. Title.
PS8559.L5494M96 2012   jC813'.54   C2012-902181-4

Cover photograph by Reza / Webistan
Cover design by Michael Solomon after a design by Alysia Shewchuk
Text design by Michael Solomon

Groundwood Books is committed to protecting our natural environment. As part
of our efforts, the interior of this book is printed on paper that contains 100%
post-consumer recycled fibers, is acid-free and is processed chlorine-free.

Printed in Canada

MIX
Paper from
responsible sources
FSC
www.fsc.org   FSC® C016245

To those who get up every morning
and face the struggle of the day.

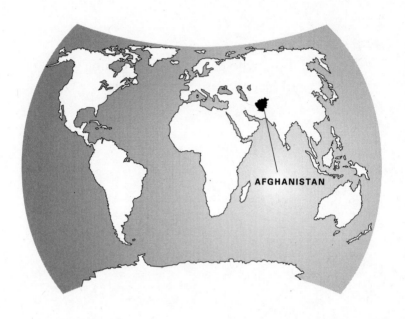

AFGHANISTAN

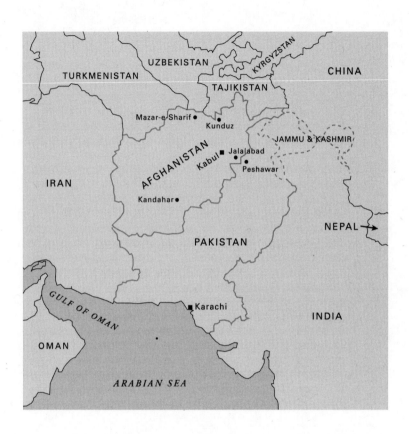

ONE

"Is your name Parvana?"

The girl in the dusty blue chador gave no response. She sat without moving on the hard metal chair and kept her eyes lowered. The cloth of the chador covered the lower half of her face.

If her mouth twitched in recognition of the English words, the uniformed man and woman staring at her could not tell.

"Is your name Parvana?"

The woman repeated the man's question, translating it into Dari, then Pashtu. Then, after a pause, into Uzbek.

The girl stayed still.

"She's not answering, sir."

"I can see that, Corporal. Ask her again."

The woman cleared her throat, then repeated the question in all three languages.

"Is your name Parvana?"

The words were louder this time, as though it were a lack of volume that kept the girl from responding.

The girl did not move and she did not answer. She

kept her eyes on a scuff mark on the floor and did not look up.

Sounds reached the little office — sounds muffled by walls and from far away. A truck engine. Boots pounding sand. A jet flying overhead. The whirl of a helicopter blade.

The girl knew there were other people around. She had seen them when they rushed her from the truck and brought her in to sit in this small room on this hard chair. She had not looked around then, either, keeping her eyes on the sand and rock of the yard, then on the cement block stairs and then on the hard gray floor of the long hallway.

"Perhaps she is deaf, sir."

"She's not deaf," the man replied. "Look at her. Does she look deaf?"

"I'm not sure ..."

"If she were deaf, she would be looking all around, trying to figure out what was going on. Is she looking around? Has she raised her head? No. Her eyes have been lowered since she was brought in, and I haven't seen her raise her head once. Trust me, she is not deaf."

"But she hasn't spoken, Major. Not a word."

"She probably said something when they grabbed her and put her in the truck. Did she scream or yell anything?"

"No, sir."

"Well, what did she do?"

The girl in the blue chador heard the sound of papers fluttering as the woman in the green army uniform read through a report.

"Sir, it says here that she stood still and waited."

"Stood still and waited." The man said the words slowly, as though he was chewing them around in his mouth. "Corporal, what is your gut telling you about her?"

There was a pause. The girl in the blue chador imagined the woman was trying to figure out what sort of answer would please the major.

"Sir, I don't have enough information to be able to form an opinion."

"Corporal, why did you join up?"

"My Spanish teacher suggested it. She said I have an ear for languages and the military could use me."

"You went to the Defense Language Institute in Monterey?"

"Yes, sir."

"You're very young. Ever hold any other job?"

"I worked in my parents' bakery."

"Bread?"

"Some bread. Cookies, squares, pies, cakes. Things like that."

"Apple turnovers?"

"Certainly, sir."

"My favorite."

"If you like, I can ask my parents to send you some."

"Thank you, Corporal. They will be stale by the time they get here, but still pretty good, I'll bet. So, a small-town bakery with a little bit of everything. And when you worked there, you did a bit of everything — baking, calling suppliers, dealing with customers?"

"Yes, sir."

"Ever get the feeling that someone is up to no good?"

"Sir?"

"Someone comes into your store, and they don't do anything bad and they don't say anything bad, but still you think, 'There's something off about this customer.' And so you watch them closely and you're glad when they leave."

"I suppose so, sir. It's a small town but bad things happen everywhere."

The man tapped his pen against the edge of the desk. He tapped for a while. The girl in the blue chador knew she would have to work hard to keep it from annoying her.

"Look at her," the man said.

There was the sound of bodies shifting in seats.

"She hasn't spoken a word and she stood still and waited to be arrested," he said. "What does that tell you?"

"I don't know, sir. Perhaps she's afraid."

"Does she look afraid?"

There was another pause.

"No, sir. She doesn't. Perhaps, though ... perhaps there is something wrong with her. Maybe she isn't smart enough to be afraid."

"You were a baker, Corporal. I worked Security. I've learned how to spot trouble. And this girl is trouble. What do we know about her?"

"Very little, sir. She was picked up in an abandoned ruin that used to be a school. We suspect that it is now being used as a staging area for the Taliban to launch attacks against us, and our intelligence gathering among the villagers seems to confirm that, although no one will speak openly. This girl was the only one there. And she had a tattered bag over her shoulder. In the bag were some papers that had the name Parvana on them. That's why we think that might be her name."

"Let me see the bag."

"Sir, I believe the analysts have it."

"Go get it. I can't wait for them to do their fine-tooth-comb thing. They'll take as much time as they get. Chase it down. Bring it back here. If they squawk, tell them it's an order."

"Yes, sir."

The girl in the chair saw the woman's army boots cross the floor and leave the office. As the door was opened, more noises came in from the outside — phones ringing, people speaking, filing cabinets opening and closing.

The girl kept her ears open and her eyes on the

floor. She knew the man at the desk was watching her. She did her best to ignore him. It was difficult. She used an old trick she had used to keep herself going when she was scared in the wilderness.

She recited multiplication tables to herself.

Nineteen times seven is one hundred and thirty-three. Nineteen times eight is one hundred and fifty-two. Nineteen times nine is one hundred and seventy-one.

She made it all the way through the twenty-eight times table before the woman's boots entered the office again. She heard the sound of someone putting her father's shoulder bag on the desk.

"This looks like it has seen better days," the man said. "Let's see what we've got in here."

He named each thing as he took it out of the bag.

"One notebook. What does this writing say?"

"Sir, that says, 'Property of Parvana. Everyone else keep out.'"

"That's just what my own teenaged daughter would have written. What language is it?"

"Dari. But we don't know that it is her notebook. She could have been scavenging or — "

"Pens," the man said. "And a copy of *To Kill a Mockingbird*, in English. What would a girl like this be doing with an American classic? But look. It's got pages torn out — even looks like someone's taken bites out of it! Why are we even trying to civilize these people?" He threw it on the desk.

The girl in the blue chador had a very hard time not jumping out of her chair, grabbing the book and hitting the man over the head with it.

She heard someone flipping through the notebook.

"Who is this girl? What is she up to?" the man asked. "Maybe she was, as you say, just scavenging. That would fit. Her clothes are covered in dust. Her feet are filthy. She looks as if she has been sleeping outside in the dirt. Was there anything else of value in that building?"

"To these people, everything is of value, sir," the woman said. "But, yes, there were other things she could have taken. A radio. Some kitchen things."

"Things she could use, in other words. Or sell. So, if she were just a scavenger, she would have taken them. Instead she takes this ratty old shoulder bag full of useless scraps of paper and one half-eaten book. No. My instincts are right. She was up to something. And we are going to get to the bottom of it. Lock her up."

The words caused a jolt of fear to zip through the girl's body.

"There is a problem, sir," the woman said. "The cells are all full of men."

"No women's cells?"

"There hasn't been a need for them,"

"Well, there's a need now. This girl isn't going anywhere."

There was another pause. The banging of the pen on the desk started up again.

"What about the brig?" the man asked after a while.

"The army brig? That's for soldiers."

"It has cells, doesn't it? Are they secure?"

"Yes, but ..."

"But what?" the man asked.

"The cells in the brig are a bit nicer than the ones we use for the Afghan prisoners."

The man laughed. "This is hardly a lucky day for this girl, Corporal. However nice the cell is, it's still a prison. One she may be in for a very long time." He picked up the telephone and punched in some numbers.

The girl in the chair tried to go back to her multiplication tables. She needed to stay calm. She needed to not let anyone know how afraid she was.

The man hung up the phone. "Done. Get her settled. We can't get anything from her if she won't talk. Get her to talk to us. Keep asking her name. Ask it over and over again until she tells it to you just to shut you up. That's all."

The woman stood up. "Yes, sir!"

She took hold of the girl's arm and led her out of the office and down the hall. Once more they were back in the sunshine. The girl was led across a yard, past a line of tanks and armored cars, past a group of soldiers doing jumping jacks, past several large gray metal buildings. They went up some steps into another building and walked down a long hallway. They stopped in front of a row of gray doors.

She heard the key turn in the lock. The door opened. She was given a little nudge and stepped into the cell. The door closed behind her.

She could tell the woman was watching her through the small window in the door. The girl kept her back against the door and didn't move.

"We can keep you locked up here for a very long time," the woman finally said, speaking softly. "Talk to me. Is your name Parvana?"

The girl remained with her back against the door. Silent.

She heard the woman's boots walk away down the hall. She stood and waited, listening hard to see if the boots would come back.

When she was sure she was alone, the girl in the dusty blue chador finally spoke.

"Yes," she whispered. "My name is Parvana."

TWO

Parvana looked around at the little room where she had landed.

It wasn't bad. It was clean. It had a narrow metal bed with a thin mattress on it. A gray blanket was folded at one end. Next to the bed a metal table was attached to the wall. Underneath was a stool that folded under the table.

The walls were smooth gray and made of metal. Parvana's eyes traveled across them and rested on a small sticker down near the floor by the bed. She knelt down for a closer look.

Port-A-Prison, she read. *The Creative Containment Specialists, for all your containment needs.*

The words were in English, which she could read. She kept reading and learned that the prison had been built in North America, in a place called Fort Wayne, Indiana. They must have folded it up like a cardboard box and packed it into a big plane to Afghanistan, then unfolded it here, on this patch of dirt in her country.

Parvana looked at the screws and bolts holding

it together. The label also said the cell had been inspected by Inspector 247.

Inspector 247 must have found everything correct, because here it was.

Parvana wondered about Inspector 247. Was it a man or a woman? Did they think about who would be held inside the gray walls they inspected? Did they have a family they went home to at night? A family who was all there because no one had been shot or had stepped on a land mine or just got too tired to keep on living? When they were younger, did they dream about becoming a portable-prison inspector?

It must be a good job, one with some authority. They got to say, "This cell is good, send it off," or, "This cell has problems. Back to the factory."

At the other end of the room was a toilet with a sink on top. Parvana gently touched the tap.

Water came out! She had running water! She let it flow over her fingertips.

A piece of paper above the sink told her that wasting water would result in further punishment. She quickly shut off the tap and waited for the boots in the hallway. None came.

"What more can they do to me?" she whispered.

She turned the tap back on and splashed water on her face. She turned it off again when she was done. Not because she was afraid of being punished, but because this was a dry part of the country, and water was never a thing to be wasted. And while the prison may have come from America, the water came from Afghanistan. It belonged to her.

The bed looked inviting. Oh, to stretch out on a bed that belonged just to her, in a room with a closed door and running water! But she could not allow herself to sleep, not yet. Not until she knew what was going on.

She stood for a while by the door, looking for any opening that might let her peer out into the hallway. There was none. There was a metal screen, but the covering to it slid open on the other side of the door. Her captors could slide it back and look at her whenever they wanted, but she could not look at them.

When she finally permitted herself to sit down on the bed, she perched on the edge, half sitting and half ready to spring into action if the situation called for it. The bed had a metal ledge to hold the mattress in place.

She was tired and scared, but this was the first time in her life that she had had a room of her own, and she wanted to enjoy it as much as possible.

If she had been asked to design this room — if Inspector 247 had asked her opinion — Parvana would have had something to say about the color.

Blue, she thought. A bright blue, the color of the sky on a brilliant winter morning before the clouds rolled in from the mountains. She would add a few splashes of red here and there. A cheerful red, like the red of the fancy shalwar kameez she had to part with when she was a child because her family needed the money.

That was years ago, but she could still see it fluttering away through the market — a bright splash of color in an otherwise dismal place. Her last splash of childhood, sold to a stranger.

She would have designed the bed in such a way that it could be folded against the wall, giving her room to walk or dance or do exercises. She was used to doing hard physical exercises at school and would like to keep on doing them if she could.

And, of course, the window would be bigger. It would look out over an orchard and a river, and beside it would be a door that she could open and walk through whenever she wanted.

But then it wouldn't be a jail cell.

The bed became a little too comfortable, and her chin started to drop to her chest. She brought it up with a jerk, then stood up. She stamped her feet a little to wake herself up.

She needed to stay awake. She needed to be alert for whatever was coming.

Everyone had heard the stories. Everyone knew somebody who knew somebody who had disappeared behind the walls of one of these places. Sometimes they came out again, angry and vowing revenge. Sometimes they came out trembling and scuttled off into the corners to mumble to them-

selves. Everybody knew somebody who knew somebody. It was a secret that everybody knew.

What went on behind prison walls was bad. Parvana had seen the scars, the marks of torture. The
peddler who pushed his cart through the refugee
camp each day would show his scars to anyone who
tried to buy a pot or a brush from him.

"This is not the Taliban," he said. "This is from
the ones who saved us from the Taliban. Who will
save us from the saviors?"

Parvana had heard his story three times, since she
often took care of the housekeeping for the family.
On and on he went, showing his battered wrists and
ankles over and over.

"I'm just a peddler," he would say. "I just push a
cart. I don't know what is in the heart of the person
I sell a shoelace to. When a man buys a bar of soap,
I don't ask him if he is the devil. Why did they arrest
me? Why did they hurt me?"

The first time she heard the story, Parvana was fas-
cinated, shocked and sympathetic. She wanted to do
something for the old man. All she could think of was to
tell him to keep the change from her purchase, but she
couldn't do that because her family had so little money.
So she listened to his story until he tired of telling it,
picked up the handles of his cart and went on his way.

The second time she heard his story she also felt
sad and sympathetic, but she remembered the tongue-
lashing her mother had given her the last time for

standing around and talking instead of working. So she kept looking for a spot in the man's story when she could politely back away.

The spot never came. He talked and talked, showing his scars, describing his pain and demanding answers: "Why was this done to me? I am nobody. Why would they do this to such a nobody?" Parvana grew frustrated that she had no answers and could not help him. She finally backed away on her own, leaving him screaming at the sky.

The third time, she pretended not to know the man. She chose the tea and thread that she needed, looked down at the dirt and paid without speaking. She could feel the loneliness coming off him in waves, and she shut herself against it.

She did not want to end up like the peddler. She did not want to end up angry and howling for revenge. Who would she get revenge from, anyway? How far back in time would she need to go before she was satisfied? Did a word like revenge have any real meaning in a country like Afghanistan?

Parvana doubted it.

To howl for revenge would be a waste of time. And enough of her time had been wasted already.

She didn't want to lose her mind behind these walls. Afghanistan already had plenty of lost minds, floating like invisible balloons in the air above the land, leaving behind empty-minded people moaning and lonely in the dirt.

"How do I come out of this?" she asked herself in a whisper.

She had to believe they would one day let her out.

She could not admit that it was quite likely they would not.

After all she had been through she knew only one thing for sure.

She knew she could not trust them.

All she could trust was herself.

THREE

They came in the night.

Parvana was ready for them.

The metal bar of the bedframe stuck into the back of her thighs while she sat on the edge of the bed. The pain helped to keep her awake.

But it pressed on the nerves in her legs and made her feet numb. When the two uniformed women, flanked by men with guns drawn, burst into her cell and each grabbed an arm to take her out, her legs buckled underneath her, forcing the guards to drag her along the corridor.

"Stand up!" one of them ordered.

Parvana gave no sign that she understood their English. It wouldn't have mattered. Her feet were quite asleep.

"This is ridiculous," the other guard said. "I didn't sweat through Basic Training to deal with stubborn teenagers."

A silent signal must have passed between the two guards because they both released their grip on

Parvana at the same time. She dropped to the floor like a sack of rice.

"On your feet!"

Parvana stayed where she was.

I'm not going to help you, she thought. She was fine on the floor. She'd had many a good night's sleep on rougher surfaces.

She was picked up again and the drag continued.

Parvana's chador came off. Now she had no way to hide her face. She didn't like that they would be able to see her.

She was hauled back into the little office and dumped onto the same hard chair. She was surrounded by boots and legs and torsos.

Nineteen times seven is …

She was too nervous to work it out, so she went for something easier. Two times two is four. Two times three is six. Two times four is eight.

She multiplied and she breathed. She got herself under control.

"There's an awful lot of people in here for one little girl."

Parvana heard the voice of the man who had questioned her earlier.

"Sir, she gave us some trouble," one of the guards said.

"Anything you can't handle, soldier?"

"No, sir. No problem, sir."

"Good. Return to your duties."

"Yes, sir."

Parvana watched the pairs of boots march out of the room.

She suddenly remembered a counting song she had used to teach the young ones. It was a good song because they learned counting and English at the same time.

The ants came marching two by two,
Hurrah, hurrah.

Parvana had to work really hard not to smile. She had no chador to cover her.

"So you've decided to let us see your face, have you?" The man said it in English, without the interpreter in the room, so he was talking more to himself than to Parvana. "We want to show respect for your culture while we are guests in your country, but I find it awfully hard to talk to someone when I can't see their face."

The feeling was starting to come back into Parvana's feet and legs. It was a mixture of tingling and pain. It was not pleasant, but Parvana welcomed it. It gave her something to concentrate on.

The interpreter entered the little room. "I found this in the hall."

Parvana could see a corner of her chador, trailing on the floor.

"Do you want me to give it to her?"

"Do you want your head covering?" the man asked.

The interpreter repeated the words in Dari, Pashtu and Uzbek. Parvana concentrated on the pain in her legs.

"She seems fine without it," he said. "If she wants it, she'll ask for it. Perhaps, in exchange, she'll tell us her name."

The woman translated what he said.

"You know what?" said the man. "I think you speak Dari. That's the language in those notebooks we found, so that's the language we're going to use. Corporal, repeat this one last time in all three languages. Tell her this is her last chance. If she doesn't speak Dari, she has to let us know now. We've given her a nice long rest. Now she has to give us something. I'm tired of pussy-footing around."

The interpreter stumbled over the translation of "pussy-footing" and finally came up with "wearing the feet of a cat." Parvana looked at the army boots and managed not to laugh.

She concentrated on her multiplication tables.

They all sat in silence for a long time.

There was a sudden loud bang. She jumped in her chair.

"So. You can hear."

The man picked up the thick book he had dropped on the floor.

"You're not deaf. You are refusing to talk to us."

While he talked, the woman translated. Parvana blocked out the woman's voice and concentrated on the man's. Her English was not as good as she wanted it to be. She had to pay attention to be able to understand him. The mental effort kept her calm.

"Why are you refusing to talk? That's the first question we have to answer. Are you refusing to talk because you're an ignorant country girl, too ignorant even to protest at being locked up? Or are you a person to worry about? Is your name Parvana?"

The question about her name again came at her fast. She wasn't prepared and almost answered it. But she managed to hold her tongue.

"You're wasting my time, little girl, and you need to start talking. Although you are hardly a little girl. How old do you think she is, Corporal? Fifteen?"

"Not more than that, sir."

"She'll age fast in this country. I've seen women who are twenty look forty, and women who are forty look seventy. The average woman here lives only to be forty-six. Did you know that, Corporal? Forty-six."

The poor corporal wasn't sure what she should translate and what was simply the major making conversation, so she translated everything. Words came out of her mouth in Dari moments after the man said them in English. To Parvana it sounded like two similar but different recordings being played, one just ahead of the other. When it happened in short spurts, it was okay. When it went on for a while, it made her brain a little dizzy.

"What are the other names we got from those pages?" the man asked.

"Sir, I made a list."

"Let me see it."

There was the sound of sliding paper.

"Is your name Shauzia?"

Parvana kept her eyes focused on the floor. She thought of her friend, swift-footed and determined, hair cropped short against her scalp, running around the marketplace with a tray of tea cups. She pictured her friend's face, laughing, crying and angry, pinched in concentration as she counted up her money, calm and dreamy as she planned her trip to France.

But she kept her breathing shallow and even, not giving anything away.

"Is your name Nooria?"

Older sister Nooria, bossy and sure of herself, with beautiful long hair. Nooria could boss the both of you right out of here, Parvana thought.

"Is your name Maryam?"

Little sister Maryam, bouncy, clever, exasperating.

"Is your name Leila?"

Parvana was glad she had no tears left. It meant she could hear the name of the little girl who had died in the minefield and not react.

I'm turning to stone, she thought. I'm sitting here turning to stone.

"Is your name Asif?"

"Sir, Asif is a boy's name."

"You sure? All right. Is your name Hassan?"

"Also a boy's name, sir."

"What about this one? Ali?"

"Also a boy's name."

"It's also a girl's name," the man said. "Haven't you ever heard of Ali McGraw? *Love Story*? Steve McQueen's girlfriend? Don't you ever watch old movies?"

"Sir, in Afghanistan, Ali is only a boy's name."

"Well, ask her anyway. Maybe she uses it as a nickname."

"Is your name Ali?"

Parvana wished they would shut up. Couldn't they just accept that she wasn't going to answer their questions and let her go? After they gave back her shoulder bag, of course.

"Any names left?"

"Just one. But I don't think it would apply."

"Ask it anyway. We need to get some sort of reaction out of her."

"Is your name Mrs. Weera?"

Parvana almost laughed out loud at that one.

I'm not Mrs. Weera, she thought. And you're very lucky that I'm not.

They all sat in silence again for a good long while.

Then the man said, "Take her chair away."
Parvana was made to stand.
And stand.
And stand.

FOUR

Parvana stood in the hot sun with the other students, listening to the government man drone on and on.

"The opening day of a new school is a grand new beginning for all of us," he was saying. "The hard work we have done has paid off in this glorious accomplishment."

The hard work we have done? Parvana had never seen that man before in her life, and here he was, claiming credit for work that wasn't his.

Her family had done the work. All the crazy members of it — those who had been born into it and those who had joined.

She had been the one to find the building. She found it when she was out on a walk to escape for a short while from the camp for internal refugees she had landed in. Her mother had been the one to decide they should take it over, and raised such a ruckus with local officials and the military that they gave her the ruined building just to shut her up. Nooria was the one who connected with organizations that could give them funding to turn the rubble into a school. Asif repaired the old water pump and found a broken generator that he also fixed. Even Maryam helped clean, and Hassan helped put things on shelves.

They had built this place, with the help of many other hands.

The government man hadn't lifted a finger.

Mother must be furious, Parvana thought, and she looked over at the tall woman with the straight back and the head held high. She was sitting on the platform with the guests from the military and the foreign agencies that had given them money.

If her mother was feeling any anger at the government man, she certainly wasn't showing it. She looked happy and maybe just a little nervous that her students wouldn't behave properly.

Nooria would certainly be annoyed. Parvana's older sister was always crabby about something.

Her sister was sitting with the other teachers, all wearing the dark blue chador that marked them as staff. They were all young women who had taken a crash course on how to be a teacher. Nooria, too, looked happy and not angry.

Of course she's happy, Parvana thought. She has a whole classroom of kids to boss around now, instead of just Maryam and me.

Maryam was Parvana's youngest sister. She was standing in the first row of students, directly in front of Parvana, wearing the white chador that all the students wore.

Maryam was a squirmer. She couldn't sit still for more than two minutes, always bopping around to some pop tune in her head. Mother said she was contrary, just like Parvana. Parvana thought it more likely that Maryam still had energy inside her that couldn't come out when she was kept inside their small apartment during the time the Taliban was in charge.

Parvana was supposed to keep an eye on her, but she had mostly given up on that. Maryam would settle when she was ready to settle, and not a moment before.

Parvana kept moving her eyes until they landed on Asif, sitting with the other school staff, looking like he was actually listening to the government man's silly speech. He no longer looked like the angry boy Parvana had found in a cave a little over four years before. They had wandered Afghanistan together, filthy and hungry.

Today he was wearing his good snow-white shalwar kameez. His dark hair was shining and curling around his ears. His face had filled out, no longer hollow-eyed from hunger.

He was still more fun to argue with than anyone Parvana had ever known.

On Asif's lap sat Hassan, the little boy Parvana had found in the bombed-out village. Hassan had been a baby then. Now he was ready for kindergarten. He was sitting tall and still. Only Asif could get him to behave so well.

There were two other school staff — Mr. Fahir, the chowkidar who kept control of the gate, and Mrs. Zaher, the cook.

Parvana thought about all these people, and forgot about being angry.

She was startled out of her thoughts by the sound of applause. The government man had finally stopped talking. Mother, as the headmistress of the new school, stepped forward. Together they unveiled the sign with the school's name:

Leila's Academy of Hope

Parvana blinked to get rid of the tears she felt in her eyes. It had been her idea to name the school after the tiny girl with the big imagination. Parvana and Asif were going to plant a flower garden in her memory, too.

Maryam took two steps forward from the group and sang the Afghan national anthem, clear and true. She was always singing along to the radio, and when the radio wasn't on, she sang Afghan and American pop songs from memory. She sang the national anthem as if she was more proud of her singing ability than she was of her country, but so what? Her little sister could count on her voice. Afghanistan still had to prove itself.

Maryam finished strong, everyone applauded, and photographers took her picture. The formal part of the ceremony was over.

While tea was prepared, Parvana took a group of parents on a tour of the school.

"Here is the kindergarten room," she said, opening the door into a small, bright, colorful room with mats on the floor and a few toys along the side. "Children up to the age of six are in this room. They will learn songs, how to wash their hands, basic counting, how to write their names, things like that."

"Will they learn how to pray?" a man in the back of the group asked.

"Um, yes, they will." Parvana was surprised by the question and did not have a smooth answer ready. "They will also get three meals a day, prepared in the school kitchen ..."

"And who will teach them to pray?" The man at the back barked the question at her.

"We have excellent teachers on staff."

"Women! Women will teach them to pray?"

"Um ... we will invite the imam to come to teach them," Parvana replied, but she didn't feel good about her answer. It felt like she was agreeing with the man, that women teachers were not good enough.

"We will also be teaching first-aid and simple nursing," Parvana said. "Real medical professionals will be teaching us. The plan is that every girl will have good knowledge of basic health care by the time she graduates. It could help her get a job and will be good for her family and community."

They moved on to another classroom.

"We have grades one to three in this room," she said.

This was the class her sister Nooria was going to teach. It had three big tables for the students to sit around to do their lessons. The tables could be pushed to the side to make room for games and exercises and story time.

"They will learn to read and write and do simple arithmetic. They will learn about the animals and plants of Afghanistan, the names of the provinces and about other countries, and how to be a good citizen."

Parvana knew all this because Nooria had talked of little else for months, poring over every education book she could find and having long discussions with their mother.

"We're starting from scratch," Nooria would say. "Everything that was here before is no good now. It all led to war and those terrible years. We have a chance to create a system that will raise a new type of Afghan child, a child with high expectations and with the confidence to rebuild the country."

She would go on and on about it, like she was making a speech — particularly when there were dishes to be washed or water to be fetched. But that was Nooria. Years of war had not made her act less bossy or feel less superior.

Parvana found it annoying, but she was also a little relieved. In a world where everything could fall apart very quickly, Nooria being bossy was almost comforting.

"Right down the hall is the middle-grade classroom," Parvana said, and they looked into the room that was for grades four, five and six. "We're calling the classes grades, but really they are age groups. It's likely that everyone will be starting at the same level since all the schools have been closed for so long."

After that, Parvana led the group to the dining hall, which also held the few shelves of books that made up the school library. This would be the room where Parvana and the few other girls her age would study. They had different levels of education. Some had only got to the second grade, but they would feel better if they learned with girls their own age, rather than with the little kids.

"What are these books?"

The same man was complaining again. He held up a tattered copy of *Alphabeasts*, a picture book with the letters of the English alphabet represented by animals.

"We don't have many books yet," Parvana said. "We have some that were donated. Most of those are in foreign languages."

She remembered the excitement everyone had felt when the boxes of books came in on an army truck, donated by some people in Canada. Her favorite so far was a collection of American poetry. The language was simple, so she could understand the words even if she couldn't understand the poem. And the poems were short. She could usually get through a whole poem before her mother yelled at her to stop reading and get back to work. Parvana had helped to set up their tiny library, and had arranged each book on the shelf as if it were made of the finest china.

"We hope to get books in our own language soon."

"Look at these pictures! Disgraceful!"

He was holding the book open at one of Parvana's favorite pictures in the whole book, M is for Mandrill. It was of a monkey waiting for a phone call.

"We are lucky to have any books at all," one of the other parents said, taking the book from him. "I never went to school, and now my daughter is going to this fine place. And I'll be sure to tell her to look at this book. It will make her laugh, and I want her to laugh."

He replaced the book carefully on the shelf.

The tour continued. Parvana showed them the kitchen and explained that all the students would take turns helping to prepare the meals and keep the school clean.

"And this is the Wall of Achievement."

It had been Parvana's idea to turn the large, blank wall in the dining hall into a place where girls could post pictures and stories about Afghan women and girls doing great things. Parvana had taken complete charge of it, going through the newspaper each morning and clipping out stories about girls winning science competitions or women joining the police force. In big letters she copied out phrases from the new constitution that protected women's rights.

In the center of the board was a photo and article about Mrs. Weera, her old friend from Kabul who had just been elected to the new Afghan parliament.

"When classes get going, girls can put up their calligraphy or a map they have drawn well or a perfect arithmetic paper. Anything they have worked hard on and done a good job with," Parvana told the group.

"Doesn't that just encourage them to be proud?" the complaining man asked.

"Yes," Parvana said.

The next stop was the playground.

"Everyone will get at least one hour of exercise each day," she said. "Plus recess and games. We have basketball, volleyball and football, although our yard is too small for real football games. The little ones will have lots of running games."

"Girls should not do this," the man said. "It is immodest. It is forbidden."

Parvana held her tongue and led the group across the yard to the workshop at the back.

This was Asif's territory.

He was sitting at his workbench, sharpening some

old tools that had been donated. He had changed out of his good shalwar kameez and had his work apron over his regular clothes. He picked up his crutch and stood respectfully when the group entered.

Parvana introduced him.

"This is Asif. He teaches carpentry, machine shop, car repair — all mechanical things."

The complaining man launched into a rant about how these were not appropriate things for girls to study. But he was cut off by Asif, who said politely, "Perhaps you would prefer to send your daughter to another school."

"My daughter will never go to school!" the man exclaimed. "Her place is in the home."

"This is a day for the parents of students," Asif said. "Would you like me to show you the way out?"

The man glared at Asif for a long moment. Then, with a huff, he swept himself out of the workshop.

Asif continued as if nothing had happened.

"Eventually we will be doing small repairs for people in the community," he said. "We want to give students work experience and also say thank you to the village for letting us have a school here."

He wrapped up his talk. Parvana showed the parents the vegetable garden that she had already spent hours digging and planting, and the latrines, which were whitewashed and spotless. She had also spent hours digging these outhouses, making them extra deep to cut down on the flies and the smell.

She led the group back to the party just in time to help serve pieces of cake.

A representative from a French charity was among the foreign guests. Parvana made her way over to him with her tray of desserts. She waited patiently for him to finish his conversation with the government man. It was a long wait.

Finally, the government man was led away to meet another foreign guest. Parvana moved in.

The Frenchman took a piece of cake and looked surprised when Parvana didn't leave.

"Are there really lavender fields in France?" she asked him.

"Lavender fields? Yes, of course. The most beautiful places! All purple. And the scent! So sweet!"

"Have you ever seen them?"

"Yes, of course."

Parvana felt foolish asking her next question, but she couldn't stop herself.

"Have you ever seen a little girl sitting in one? Well, she wouldn't be a little girl anymore. She would be my age. I know you probably haven't. But have you?"

He hadn't.

Even if her friend Shauzia had made it out of Afghanistan, there was little chance she had gone all the way to France. And even if she had and had found a lavender field to sit in, she probably wouldn't still be sitting there, years later.

But Parvana could see it in her mind — Shauzia, just as she last saw her when they said goodbye in Kabul. She would be sitting among the purple flowers, with the sun shining and everything quiet.

Parvana could only hold that picture in her head for a moment before it disappeared, and she wondered, for perhaps the millionth time, what had happened to her friend.

When the reception was over, the chairs back in place, the guests and students gone, Parvana sat at one of the dining-hall tables with her family — her mother, her sisters and her two adopted brothers.

Everyone was busy with some little project. Mother was working on the finances. Nooria was working on her lesson plans. Maryam was drawing pictures of dresses she would like to wear when she became a singing star. Asif was trying to teach Hassan how to write his name.

It was peaceful. Everyone was all right.

Maybe Shauzia *is* in a lavender field in France, Parvana thought, but it couldn't be any nicer than right here, right now.

"I don't want to be anywhere else," she said out loud.

"What are you babbling about?" Asif asked.

Parvana almost hugged him.

FIVE

They made Parvana stand for a very long time.

Her back was two inches from the wall, and whenever she appeared to be leaning against it, they would yell at her to stand up straight. She had to keep pretending not to understand. When they got tired of yelling, they would move her away from the wall themselves.

The man and woman in uniform kept staring at her as she stood. Every now and then they would ask, "What is your name?" and "What were you doing in that school?"

She didn't answer, and the periods of silence grew longer and longer.

To pass the time, the man started to clean his weapon. Parvana watched him take apart the gun, polish it up and put it back together again.

Asif could do that better than you, she thought, although he wouldn't have wasted his time on guns. Engines were his thing. He had started learning about engines in the refugee camp he and Parvana had ended up in. He hung around the clinic and helped take care of the truck. Every foreigner he met, he asked about their car, asked to see under the hood and asked if they needed someone to keep the car clean. He even managed to earn a little bit of money that way.

And he learned to read.

Parvana remembered the conversation they had about it.

They were sitting on a small hill overlooking the camp.

"Your mother says if I'm going to be part of your family," Asif said, "I have to learn to read."

"That sounds like something Mother would say," Parvana replied.

"You probably think you're really special, with all that reading and writing you do."

"You should try it," Parvana said.

"You say that because you think I won't be able to, don't you? You'd love it if I tried and couldn't do it. You want to keep all the reading and writing for yourself. You'd probably hate it if I could read and write as well as you do."

Parvana waited. She knew what was coming.

"I'm going to learn," Asif said. "Just to annoy you."

He stood up right then and went back down to the camp to find Parvana's mother and get his first lesson.

A soldier brought food into the little room and

gave it to the major and the interpreter. Parvana could smell the grilled meat from the hamburgers they bit into. They didn't offer her any.

"Talk," the man said. "Talk, then eat."

Parvana kept silent. She'd been hungry before.

The questions started up again after they finished eating.

"What is your name? Who are your friends? What were you doing in that school? Why won't you talk to us? What are you hiding?"

Parvana closed her ears. She tried to send her mind somewhere else. She tried to think about how exciting it was to wake up early each morning at the school and find a quiet place to read before her mother got up and the work started. She tried to think about how much she loved seeing the students come to school every morning. She would often stand at the gate with Mr. Fahir, the chowkidar, and say hello as they arrived, all clean and brushed, their white chadors washed overnight and pressed under their mattresses.

The girls would sometimes come on their own in a group, walking together for protection against the stares and insults. Usually they came with an adult — a mother or father or aunt or uncle — whoever was taking care of them. The parent would watch them go through the gate and keep watching long after the girl had gone inside.

Parvana knew without asking — she just knew

— that the parents were wishing they could go to school, too. And why wouldn't they? Inside the school gates everything was clean. Students cleaned it every day, washing the dust off the windowsills and the footprints off the floor. There was always the scent of cooking or nan baking. The place was bright, painted with the cheeriest assortment of colors Mother could find. The students had helped with that, too, since knowing how to paint was a skill that might earn them money one day.

No one yelled inside the school, unless it was to cheer someone on at games. There was always the sound of singing, and the walls were quickly covered with the students' art work.

Parvana both wanted and didn't want the parents to come in and be a part of it all. She wanted them to have the opportunity. Between the Soviet occupation, the civil war and the Taliban, probably none of them had ever gone to school.

But adults were unpredictable. They liked to make trouble, and Parvana had already had a lifetime of that.

"I know you are starting to feel some pain," the major said. "It's hard to stand in one place for a long time. Your back is aching. Your legs are getting sore and probably starting to swell. You probably need a latrine break, too. And I want you to have one. I want you to have a good meal and a good rest and no more worries. All you have to do is talk to me."

He moved closer so that his face was just two inches from Parvana's. She kept her eyes down but she could feel his breath on her. It was sour. She could smell the onions that had been on his hamburger.

He dropped his voice to a whisper. The interpreter moved in close and whispered her translation.

"Tell us we've made a mistake," he said. "Tell us you don't know anything. Speak one word. Just one! Any word you want, and you can rest and eat. And if you can't talk, then rap your knuckles on the wall."

He tapped the wall next to Parvana's head.

"I know you can hear me," he whispered. "I'm pretty sure you understand me. Now I need you to talk to me. One word. Say 'stop' or 'flower' or 'puppy' or 'grenade.' Say just one word. Talk to me, and I'll let you rest."

Parvana kept silent. She tried to breathe shallow to avoid the smell of sour onions.

And then he yelled, right into her face.

"Talk to me!"

It was a loud yell, a parade-ground yell, a yell designed to scare the enemy.

It scared Parvana. Her body jumped.

And then she'd had enough.

She closed her eyes, leaned back against the wall and fainted dead away.

SIX

"Is that all you've done?"

Mother stood beside Parvana's chair and looked down at her worksheet. It was supposed to be covered with fractions. Instead, there was one unfinished equation at the top of the page. The rest of the page held a map of the town Parvana would build if she ever got the chance, full of streams and bridges and hidden parks where a girl could get away by herself and not be bothered by anyone. She had forgotten that she was supposed to be doing arithmetic.

"Hanifa has done three worksheets. Sharifa has done four. And they have never been to school before."

Mother's voice had found its nag again after being silenced by the Taliban.

"You, who have been to school and had a teacher for a father, can't be trusted to complete a simple sheet of fractions. Stay in at recess. If you put your mind to it, you could have all those questions answered before the bell rings."

Hanifa and Sharifa smiled smugly and left the dining hall with Mother. They were two of the other teenaged girls in the school, and all they did all day — besides their schoolwork — was look at Parvana and smirk.

Parvana sat alone in the dining hall. The sound of children playing came in through the windows.

She slumped in her chair and banged the pen on the table. Then she threw the pen across the room.

Mother had no right to talk to her like that, especially not in front of the other students! She had worked so hard, helping to build the school. How was she to know that actually going to school would be so difficult?

Parts of school were easy. Reading books from the library shelves? Easy. Already her English had improved hugely, just from reading all the English books that had been donated. She loved the first-aid lessons, because she could clearly see a use for everything she was being taught. She liked knowing where everything was in the school and how to get things done. She loved it when students came and asked her questions, and she knew how to answer them.

But she hated being an ordinary student.

And she hated sitting still.

How could she be expected to sit at a table for hours, staring down at a bunch of numbers? She was used to *doing* things. She was used to working and scrounging, dodging and surviving.

Not sitting and staring.

Parvana looked down at her messed-up math assignment. Multiplying fractions. Why would anybody do such a thing? She couldn't understand it and she was tired of trying. Mother had explained it. Nooria had explained it. Even the other teachers had explained it. She still could not understand how to multiply one-third by one-fifth, or why anybody would ever want to.

She could not stay in that room any longer. She couldn't stand the thought of spending two more hours sitting with the Smirking Girls. Everything was closing in on her.

She had to get out.

So, she left.

She walked right out of the dining hall, past Mrs. Weera's face on the Wall of Achievement, out of the school and through the gate, not stopping when Mr. Fahir called after her.

Parvana walked hard, needing to move her muscles and feel her heart pound. She walked without looking around, muttering under her breath about useless fractions and her mother's unfairness.

She walked down a gravel road with fields on each side. Some of the fields were planted with opium poppies, which turned the valley green and pink when the flowers were in bloom. Rocky hills surrounded the area like the sides of a bowl.

Parvana stomped her way down the road to the village. By the time she reached the first of the shops and houses, her anger had been stomped out.

People had set up camp on the edge of the village. Some had tents. Most just had tarps stretched across boards or bags full of straw or sand. A few goats rooted through the garbage. Children in grubby clothes sat in the dirt or kicked around an old tin can.

It was a smaller version of the camp for internal refugees where Parvana had finally found her family. The remnants of that camp were not far away, but Parvana had no desire to go back there. Living that way was very hard.

After the tents came the mud houses — low square buildings made from mud bricks. Dung patties had been pressed by hand against the walls to dry in the sun. They would be used as fuel to cook meals and heat the houses. Some of the huts had little shops operating out of a window — glass cases with gum, candies, crackers and soap.

Parvana passed a baker and smelled the nan fresh from the oven. She passed a butcher, with a skinned headless goat carcass hanging on a hook and a row of goat heads on a tray in front. Next came the fruit merchants, with oranges, onions and tomatoes piled up in pyramids. Bowls of spices and stacks of nuts were sold in the stalls around the fruit next to shops of hardware and household goods.

Parvana had grown up in Kabul and spent a lot of time working in the market there. This village had a smaller, quieter version.

Maybe I could find a job here, she thought. I know enough arithmetic to count the money I earn and to figure out how much things cost. I don't need stupid fractions for that.

It would be nice to have money in her pocket again. Since the school project started, Mother handled all the money the family had, which wasn't much.

Once, Parvana asked her for some. She felt like wandering into the village to buy some dried apricots or something for a little treat.

"You don't need any money," her mother had stated. "Everything is provided for you. Besides, you're not going out in the market. You've done far too much running around the past few years. It will do you good to start settling down."

That's what I wanted, Parvana thought, as she walked by a peddler with a cart full of plastic sandals. All she had wanted, all those years, was a normal life. She wanted to sit in a school room, in clean clothes, and have her family with her.

And now that she had all that, all she could do was complain.

"What's wrong with me?" she asked out loud.

Parvana walked clear through the village and out the other side. Once more she was in barren hills, scrub grass and big sky. She knew how easy it was to get lost in the Afghan countryside, that all the hills could very quickly start to look alike.

She climbed up the nearest hill and stopped at the

top. After checking to make sure there were no scorpions or camel spiders, she sat down and leaned her back against a big rock. From here she could see the whole village and, beyond it, her new school.

Her legs ached and felt good. They did exercises every day at school, but all the push-ups and jumping jacks could not make up for her need to wander, to move through the world and see it go by.

What's wrong with me? she asked herself again.

War planes zoomed up from a valley behind her and screamed across the sky. Parvana didn't even blink. They were as common as crows. So was the sight of smoke from an explosion rising in the distance.

Someone was tasting dirt, having their eardrums explode and seeing their world torn apart.

"But not me," she said out loud. "Not today. I've had my share. It's someone else's turn."

The ground beneath her was hard but comfortable. She knew how to sleep outside. Back at the school she shared a toshak with her sisters at night. She was always squished in the middle — between Nooria, who figured she had the right to the most space, and Maryam, who never stopped squirming, not even when she was sleeping. Many nights, Parvana just gave up and slept on the floor.

They wouldn't miss me, she thought.

Building the school had been fun. She'd had a project, a purpose. But actually going to school? No, she couldn't do it. She couldn't spend the rest of her life sitting across from those two awful girls, staring down at the same page of fractions.

"I'll hire myself out as a school builder," she said to the sky. "I'll walk around the country. Whenever I come to a village without a school, I'll go to the elders and offer to design it. They'll find me a kind old widow to stay with. I'll fetch water for her and help her out in the mornings and read to her in the evenings. During the day I'll draw up plans for the school and tell the men in the village what to do. 'Put the window in so it faces the garden!' I'll say. 'Make the playground bigger. And build more shelves for that library.'"

She could see it all. The flat roof for playing, with a ledge tall enough that children couldn't fall off, where they could fly kites during the spring festival and sleep out under the stars on hot nights. The giant vegetable garden with chicken coops at one end and a big tree to read under at the other. Any student who wanted could have a little piece of garden to grow flowers.

"And they could sell the flowers in the market. Make a bit of money."

Parvana always felt more powerful with a bit of money in her pocket.

At the school's opening-day ceremony, the government man would make another long speech. This time, though, his speech would be all about Parvana, about her skills and talents, and how she was able to accomplish so very much without even knowing how to multiply fractions.

Everyone would applaud and look for Parvana so they could give her a plaque, but she wouldn't be there. She would have slipped away, and would be walking alone down the road, off to the next village, to build the next school.

"Or maybe I'll just cut my hair again," she said. "Asif has an extra shalwar kameez that would fit me. I'll take it from his room when he's at supper. Mother has scissors in her desk. I'll turn myself back into a boy, then go out into the world and get any job I can. I'll save my money and ..."

She had nowhere to go with that thought. When she was dressed as a boy, when she was younger, there was a point to earning money. She had a family to feed and a father to get out of prison.

Now what would she save for? She had a feeling that this time, simply surviving would not be satisfying. She needed a bigger dream.

What she really wanted was to build things — things people could live in that would make them feel safe and happy and ...

Part of her brain was on the verge of admitting that to do that, she would probably need to know how to multiply fractions. And a whole lot of other things.

She pushed that thought aside.

"I'll do what Shauzia did," she decided. "I'll earn money as a boy and then I'll go to France. I'll start building things there, and when we meet up at the top of the Eiffel Tower in …" — she paused to count — "sixteen years, I'll be a successful architect."

That dream was enough to make her stand up, brush the dust from her clothes and head down the hill. She held that image in her head as she headed back through the market.

All she needed to do was make a quick stop back at the school to pick up her father's shoulder bag. It was all she had left of him, and it contained all the letters she had written to Shauzia — a record of her life over the past few years. There was no way she was leaving that behind for Nooria to paw over and laugh at.

She headed down the hill and back through the village. She was deep into a daydream where she was pointing out all the design flaws in the Eiffel Tower when a man stepped in front of her and started to yell.

"Cover your head!"

Parvana stopped. "What?"

She pulled her brain out of Paris and back into Afghanistan.

"Cover your head!"

Parvana had let her chador fall into a shawl around her shoulders. She liked the feeling of air around her head and ears.

"The law says I don't have to," she said.

"The foreigners say you don't have to. We say you do!" His shouts drew the attention of other men.

"She's from that school," another man said. "All those women together. Up to no good."

"You can't just walk through our village like that," a third man yelled. "Cover up and get out."

In a matter of moments, Parvana was surrounded by men. Shouting, cursing, angry men.

"She's come from seeing her boyfriend," one of them said. "Brings her dishonor right into our village."

Parvana tried to move through them. They closed ranks. The circle of men was three, then four deep. All she could see when she looked down were sandals on big dusty feet. All she could see when she looked up were angry mouths and eyes.

Someone thumped her in the back. More thumps landed on her shoulders and arms.

They weren't full on hitting her yet, but they were certainly warming up to it.

She started to realize that she needed to be afraid.

But before she became afraid, she decided to get angry.

She took a deep breath, got herself ready, then yelled out, as loud as she could, "Get out of my way!"

In the moment of shock that followed, Parvana saw a gap in the mob and pushed through it. Then she ran.

They ran after her.

Maybe if she had walked, they would have been shamed into leaving her alone. But she had too much adrenaline rushing through her body to be able to walk away with dignity. And that adrenaline pushed her through the village. She ran like the gazelles that used to dash across Afghanistan's plains.

She ran through the market, past the goat heads and past the tents of the refugee camp. She ran out along the open dirt road toward the school.

The men chased after her.

But she outran them. They were angry but so was she, and she was young and used to moving fast.

The men threw rocks. Some of them hit her back and bounced off into the dirt. Parvana just laughed.

She turned around to show them she was laughing at them.

"You are all living in the past!" she called out, almost at the school, waving her chador in her hand and feeling her hair tangle and toss in the wind. "I am the future! And I am leaving you far behind!"

She laughed again as the men's stones failed to hit her. Then she ran the rest of the way home.

She ran right into her mother, who had been watching the spectacle from outside the gate.

"Get inside."

Parvana waited until they were behind the school walls before saying to her mother, "I'm not a child."

"That's exactly what you are," Mother said. "You have just proved it."

Mother left her and went into the dining hall.

Parvana's joy and energy drained out of her like air from a slashed tire. She followed her mother meekly.

The students were all at the tables, doing a review of the day's work. They had no place to study at home, so they did homework at the school. They would be served tea, bread, fruit and nuts before they went home.

"May I have your attention, please."

Mother was speaking.

The girls put down their pens and lifted their eyes from their work. Parvana stood against the dining-hall wall, afraid of what was about to happen.

"From now on, no one will leave the school grounds without permission," Mother said. "No one will go out or come in without first checking with me or Mr. Fahir. Is that clear?"

"Yes, Headmistress," the girls all said.

"No, Headmistress," Parvana whispered.

"Would everyone please turn around and look at the girl standing against the wall."

All heads turned and all eyes landed on Parvana.

"That girl is not allowed to use the library for three weeks," Mother declared. "If anyone sees her with a library book, report her to me. If anyone sees her and doesn't report her, there will be trouble. Does everyone understand?"

"Yes, Headmistress."

Parvana didn't need to look at Hanifa and Sharifa to know they were smirking like earthquakes.

She stayed against the wall while supper was brought in, then joined the end of the line of students winding past the nan and orange slices.

As she reached for a piece of bread, her sheet of fractions was put into her hand instead.

"Your mother says you have to do your work before you can eat," the cook said. "I'm sorry."

Parvana didn't hold it against the cook.

"I ate in the village," she said loudly, in case anyone was listening. "I won't be hungry again for a long time."

She put the page of arithmetic on top of the platter of nan and left the dining hall.

The sheet of fractions followed her around.

When she went to the latrine, it appeared on the sink. She left it there.

When she went to the room she slept in with her family, it was on top of the blankets in the cupboards.

She crumpled it into a ball and tossed it into a corner of the room.

Mother watched her do this. Then she retrieved the paper and smoothed it out.

"You have to know this," Mother said, handing it back to her. "Like it or not, you need to know how to do this. Your future depends on it. You give up on this, you will give up on the next difficult thing, and you are too smart and too strong to start giving up. So until you get it done, you don't eat and you don't sleep."

Mother folded the paper into a neat square and pressed it into Parvana's hand, folding her daughter's fingers around it.

"Go," Mother said. "Find a place to work. I have to get the young ones to bed."

She practically shoved Parvana out of the room. The door clicked shut behind her.

Parvana's first instinct was to toss the square of paper, maybe even toss it over the school wall where it would disappear forever. Then she thought of going to the kitchen, finding a match and setting the fractions on fire.

But she knew her mother. Mother probably had a drawer full of fractions, and she would take great pleasure in tormenting her daughter with them until they were both old ladies, bent over and toothless.

I'll just leave, Parvana decided. I'm all done. I've tried to fit in, but now I'm all done.

Asif had a cot in his workshop. Parvana went to the back of the yard, saw that his kerosene lamp was still lit and knocked on the door.

"Come in," he said.

Parvana opened the door. Asif was at his workbench, surrounded by little bits of metal.

"I'm fixing Hassan's toy truck," he said. "I promised him, so don't bother me."

Parvana came right to the point.

"I want you to give me your spare shalwar kameez."

"My new white one?"

"No. Your other one."

"Why?"

"None of your business."

He put down his wrench and looked at her.

"You're the biggest fool to ever walk the earth," he said.

"Shut up."

"You're going to cut your hair off and put on my clothes, and you think then that you can just be free to do what you want."

Parvana pushed past him to where his spare shalwar kameez hung from a nail on the wall.

"I'm taking this," she said. "And keep your mouth shut. After all, you owe me."

"I owe you? For what?"

"For saving your life. For finding you in that cave and for saving your life."

Asif folded his arms across his chest and looked at her.

"Yeah," he said. "I guess you're right. I guess you saved my life. Okay. I'll keep quiet. Have a good journey. I wish you every success. Good luck getting through the gate without waking Mr. Fahir."

Parvana opened the door. Then she paused and turned.

"I guess this is goodbye," she said. "I ..."

"Of course, you could stop being a fool and just do the fractions."

"Don't start."

"Really, Parvana, you already know how to do them. You can multiply in your head. I've heard you do it often enough."

"But this is different!"

"No, it isn't. You're just telling yourself some stupid story about not being able to do them. Just like you are telling yourself some stupid story about being able to dress like a boy and pass for a boy — at your age! Some religious fanatics will kill you before the week is out. They'll stone you in the street. You say you saved my life? All right. Let me return the favor. Let me show you that you already know how to do the fractions so you don't have to leave and end up dead."

Parvana started to answer back. She hesitated. Admitting that Asif was right would be almost as awful as admitting that Nooria was right. But she remembered the angry men in the market. She knew what such men were capable of.

Maybe she could head out on her own again and be all right. Maybe.

Maybe she didn't really want to try.

Parvana knew then that she had to make a real choice. If she stayed tonight, she was staying, period, through multiplying fractions and whatever fresh horror was ahead. And if she was leaving, she wouldn't be coming back.

She was about to choose her future.

"You are the most awful boy in the world," she said, tossing the shalwar kameez onto the cot.

"And you are the most awful girl."

He waggled his fingers for the sheet of fractions. Parvana handed it to him. He unfolded it, smoothed it out, and handed Parvana a pencil.

Parvana moved in closer to the workbench, looked down at the fractions, and let herself be taught.

SEVEN

Parvana woke up on her cot to the sound of some- one opening a metal flap at the bottom of her door and sliding something inside.

She lay still. She could tell that someone was still outside the door, watching her.

She was glad to be lying down. She was so com- pletely tired she didn't think she would ever get up off the cot again. All she wanted was to stare up at the ceiling and not think about anything.

"It's all right."

The person watching whispered to her through the little screen. The whisper sounded like it came from a girl.

Parvana started to sit up. Her brain was too foggy at first to remember that she wasn't supposed to be able to understand English. She remembered when she was halfway up and lay back down on the bed again.

Her heart started pounding in her chest.

She had given herself away! The sound of her heart filled the little cell, making the walls shake and loosening all the screws so properly checked by Inspector 247.

"The food," the whisper said. "It's all right. It's an MRE, the same food we get. You'll have to eat yours cold because we had to take out the thing that heats it up. But it's okay. Just open the packets."

"Have you delivered that meal yet, Private?" Parvana heard someone yell.

"All done, sir." The voice was definitely young and female.

The soldier moved away from Parvana's cell.

Parvana forced herself to stay on her cot. She went through all the multiplication tables from one through twenty-five. Then she recited the first surah of the Qur'an to herself.

Finally she could stand it no longer. It was quiet in the hall. No one was watching her. She got up, went over to the door and picked up the tray. She put it down on the little table and inspected it.

It was a bag.

They had already opened it for her.

She looked inside.

More bags.

She took one out and read the label. Cheese Tortellini in Tomato Sauce.

She didn't know what tortellini was, but she liked cheese, and she liked tomatoes.

There were lots of words on the bag and Parvana read them all. She learned where the meal had been made, what the ingredients were, and what the expiry date was. She learned how to open it, what the vitamin content was and that it contained no trans-fats.

It was dull reading, but any reading was better than none.

They should print poems on these packages, Parvana thought. Soldiers on a battlefield would probably like to have something to read. And a good poem at the right time could change a person's life.

Who would want to shoot somebody after reading "Stopping by Woods on a Snowy Evening" or "Casey at the Bat"? She'd read both in her book of American poetry and loved them.

"Hey, you!" the soldier would shout out to whoever they were supposed to be killing. "I've just read a great poem. Let me read it to you. You're going to love it!"

The army could put jokes on the food bag, she thought, or short stories. Or chapters of novels, and the soldiers could swap until they had all read the whole book.

She could picture them sitting on top of their tanks, having a meal break.

Maybe a bunch of them would get chapters from *Little Women*, and they'd be eating and sniffling when Beth died. Or they would laugh when poor Anne of Green Gables dyed her hair green.

I should send a letter to the army, she said to herself. This is a good idea. Maybe they could hire me to choose the books.

She put that thought away to amuse herself with later and looked at the rest of the bags. There was a plastic spoon, bread, sliced Georgia peaches and a chocolate brownie.

It's a trick, she thought. Why would they give me so much food? And such fancy food!

Maybe she shouldn't eat it.

The girl at the window had said it was okay. And she had whispered, which meant she probably wasn't supposed to be talking to the prisoners.

If I don't eat, I won't have the strength to get through this, Parvana told herself.

That settled it. She opened up the tortellini. She saw red tomato sauce and little round balls of pasta. She dipped her little finger in the sauce and tasted it. The tomato and spices on her tongue kicked her appetite into high gear, and she couldn't spoon the food into her mouth fast enough.

When the tortellini was all gone, and she had scraped out as much of the sauce as she could with her spoon, she opened the edges of the bag and licked up all the rest of it.

She sat back and sighed. She could feel the energy coming back into her body. She'd be all right. She could do this.

She took a closer look at the ripped-open bag. If she took the plastic foil lining away, she would have a sheet of paper. Although she had no pen — and no way of even imagining how she would get one — it felt good to know she had some paper.

She stacked the remaining food on the little shelf above the table to eat later and got to work taking apart the bag. It was delicate work. She didn't want to rip the paper. It kept her calm and busy, and for a while she was something like happy.

They didn't come for her again. They left her alone for some time.

Meals came now and then, and once, a soldier came right into the cell and took away the remains of the old meals. By then, Parvana had four sheets of bag paper smoothed out and hidden under her mattress. She expected them to find the paper and take it away, but it gave her something to do.

Parvana kept track of the days by watching the light change through the little window high up on the cell wall.

This window was wider than it was high and not much of either. Most of it was covered with narrow metal slats that were tilted in a way that made it hard for anyone to see in or out. A bit of fresh air got in, making the cell cold at night.

Parvana discovered that by standing with her right foot on the cot and her left foot on the table, she could see out the window. Her view was chopped up by the shutters, but she could see the sky and the rocky hills in the distance. Close up, she could see trash bins, sheds and several layers of razor wire to close everything in. She could stick her fingers through the gaps in the shutters and wiggle them in the sunshine. She stood there for as long as she could keep her balance, looking out at the world.

On the third day of being left alone, the cover over the door grate slid open.

"Come over to the door."

It was the young private again, but this time she spoke loudly.

"Prisoner, come to the door."

Parvana was sitting on the side of the bed. She did not respond.

The door was unlocked. The young private had another female soldier with her. They each took one of Parvana's arms.

They tried to lift her to her feet. Parvana gripped the side of the bed. She felt safe in her cell. She did not want that man to yell at her again.

"Drag her," one soldier said.

"She's just a kid."

"She's not a kid. She's a terrorist."

One of the soldiers knelt down beside her.

"We're just taking you to get a shower," she said quietly. "It's just a shower. I'll be with you the whole time. Don't worry. I'm the woman who brings you your meals. You know you can trust me."

"She doesn't speak English. You gotta talk to her in Arab."

"Shut up. If she doesn't understand the words, she understands the tone."

The two soldiers kept up their arguing while they led Parvana out of the cell and to a small shower room at the end of the row of cells. She was handed a bit of soap and some shampoo and told to go behind a curtain and shower. They also handed her clean clothes — a pair of green army pants, green T-shirt and a long-sleeved green shirt.

"Your clothes will be washed and returned to you," they told her, but she didn't care. Her school was gone. She didn't need her school uniform anymore.

Parvana took as long in the shower as she dared. The water was cool, the soap smelled good, and the lather felt soft in her hair.

She rinsed off and put on the clean clothes. Then they led her back to her cell.

The cell had been cleaned. The floor was still damp from the mop and the medicinal smell of disinfectant hung in the air. Clean sheets and blankets were folded and stacked on the end of the bed.

Her pieces of paper were on top of her bed.

She got the message.

Nothing was safe.

EIGHT

" When someone is cut, there are three important things to do. Put pressure on the wound to stop the bleeding, clean the wound and cover the wound. This is to prevent infection and promote healing. To clean the wound, place the injury under clean running water..."

Parvana stopped reading. If that was the only way to clean a wound, all of Afghanistan was doomed to die of horrible infections.

She looked up from her page of notes and out at the faces of the thirty-six girls crowded into Nooria's classroom. Most were crammed in two to a seat. Parvana and the other older girls had begun to receive instruction in first-aid and basic nursing from a Canadian army nurse. They had been told to share what they had learned with the younger students.

Nooria's class was listening politely, but Parvana was boring herself, and she was sure she was boring the students as well.

"They won't remember much," the nurse said. "But they'll come away with the idea that there are things they can do to keep themselves healthy. That's a good first step."

Plus, there were stories in the newspapers about schools being attacked by the Taliban, bombed or burned down. If that happened at Leila's Academy of Hope, Parvana wanted everyone to be all right. That meant everyone had to know how to take care of themselves and each other.

The school had been open for a few months. Every day more families tried to enroll their daughters. Community members came in to teach cooking and embroidery and how to dry herbs for teas and seasonings. One of the teachers had a relative who knew how to distill rose petals into perfume. Another knew something about keeping bees for honey.

Mother was starting to think that one day the school could earn money to cover at least some of its costs. For now it was enough that the students came, learned something and went home well fed.

There were a few problems. They had a generator but very little fuel. The power was severely rationed and revolved around when Mother needed to recharge her cell phone, not when Parvana wanted to read. Many of the students only ate at school. Their families were poor and at home the food went to those who did not get to eat in school. The children were always ravenous when they arrived back in class after the weekend.

Mother was trying to stretch the food budget so they could send a bit of food home with the girls at the end of each week.

But the Wall of Achievement was getting crowded, with perfect arithmetic papers, samples of good calligraphy and a new section, Student of the Week, for a student who had worked really hard or done a good deed. The student got her name on the wall, and Mother sent a glowing letter home to the girl's family.

Vegetables were growing in the garden, the hens were laying eggs, and when the Afghan flag was raised each morning, the girls belted out the national anthem in loud, clear, proud voices.

As she stood in front of Nooria's classroom, Parvana could see that reading from her notes wasn't teaching anybody anything. The girls were polite, but she was putting them to sleep. Even Nooria was nodding off.

Parvana shook her head and laughed out loud. She put her notes face down on the desk.

"Who here has had a cut?" she asked.

The students woke up and put their hands in the air.

"And what comes out of your body when you have a cut?"

"Red," said one student.

"Blood," said the girl beside her.

"Red blood." Parvana put the two answers together. "Some people panic when they see blood, but we won't, will we? Because we will know what to do. Who here would like to know what to do when they see someone with a cut on their hand and blood coming out?"

All the hands went up.

That's when Parvana decided to enjoy herself.

"I'm going to ask your teacher to be the patient." She put a chair at the front of the room and motioned to Nooria to sit on it.

Nooria glared at her, but she didn't know how to refuse.

Parvana lifted her sister's hand and drew a mark on it with a felt pen.

"Your teacher has cut herself," Parvana said. "Everyone gather around and I'll show you what to do."

She had her practice first-aid kit with her, with hand-made gauzes and bandages. She showed the students how to clean the wound and wrap it with a clean piece of cloth.

With her hand wrapped up, Nooria started to rise.

Parvana put her hand on her sister's shoulder. She was just getting started.

"Oh, dear," she said. "Your teacher has broken her arm."

The girls watched in fascination as Parvana folded

a large square of fabric into a triangle and knotted it into a neat sling.

"But what if you don't have a large square?" Parvana asked them. "Maybe you just have a narrow scarf. Here's how you can use the scarf to make another type of sling."

Parvana used the scarf from around her own neck to bind up Nooria's other arm.

"Oh, dear," Parvana said. "There's been a terrible dust storm and your teacher has injuries to her eyes."

"That's enough for today," Nooria said, but she was drowned out by the enthusiasm of her students.

"You can keep the injuries from getting worse by binding the eyes shut until you can take her to a doctor," Parvana said, happily plopping a square of gauze over each eye and winding bandages around her sister's head.

"The more secure the bandages, the better," Parvana told the students, criss-crossing the bandage so that Nooria could not move her jaw.

For once, her sister could not utter a word.

It was a most sublime moment.

The bell rang for morning break.

"There's the bell," Parvana said. "Who wants juice?"

The girls bounced out of the classroom. Parvana lingered in the doorway for a moment.

She knew she'd pay for this later. She might even regret it.

But, for the moment, she felt like dancing.

And dance she did.

She danced all the way out of the school and into the courtyard, and she kept dancing, in her head, all through the lecture from Mother, the fury from Nooria, and the chore upon chore she was made to do as punishment — the hours of gardening, cleaning the latrines, scrubbing the kitchen and shoveling out the hen-house.

She worked and sweated and strained and ached, and for two whole weeks she didn't have a moment to call her own.

But she didn't regret a thing.

NINE

Parvana struggled to keep track of the days.

It was difficult. The bright ceiling light was on all the time. Meals came and went at weird intervals — sometimes after a brief time, sometimes after a long stretch.

She was taken out of her cell at all times of the day and night. One day she was made to sit in the little room with a guard watching her for what seemed like a very long time, taken back to her cell for a short while, then bang! They burst through the door to take her out again, back to the same little room, the same silent guard, the same endless, dragging hours.

Parvana suspected she had been taken back to her cell so that the guard could eat some lunch and go to the latrine, but of course she could never ask anyone about it.

She would sit on the hard chair in silence for such a long time that she started to nod off. Then the guard would bang a baseball bat against the wall next to her head. She would jolt awake and open her eyes, her heart pounding in her chest.

They would keep this up until she was so tired that her legs felt like they were full of crawling worms. Then they would take her back to her cell. She would collapse on the cot. They would leave her alone just long enough for her to be able to stop her exhausted body from twitching and slide into sleep. Then the cell door would bang open again and they would haul her back out to sit in the hard chair.

The guards who took her from the cell were women. None of the male guards touched her, and Parvana was grateful for that. The men were large and fit and looked like they could really hurt her if they wanted to.

The women soldiers were strong, too. Walking close to them as they gripped her arms was like walking next to creatures made of iron and steel. But she was hoping they wouldn't go out of their way to hurt her. No woman had ever hit her. She couldn't say the same about men. She had been hit many times by men. Some of the men had been with the Taliban. Other men had not been with the Taliban but thought they could hit her anyway.

But she didn't relax around the women. She had seen the photos from Abu Ghraib of female soldiers doing horrible things to Iraqi prisoners. Women could torture people as well as men if they wanted to.

That was one of the things Parvana thought about as she sat in the chair. She grabbed hold of any train of thought that might keep her calm and entertained.

Otherwise, all she could focus on was pain, fear, loneliness and exhaustion.

Her thoughts on women and torture went like this. Women in the West could choose to do anything they wanted. So why would they choose to do that?

And how did a woman train to be a torturer? Did she study human anatomy, the way Parvana had in science class, to learn which nerve endings were the most sensitive and which muscles could take the most beatings? Did they practice on dolls? Did they listen to recordings of someone screaming for hours on end so that they would not be bothered when they heard it for real?

She went through that long list of thoughts, examining each one from different angles. After that, she started to wonder whether or not she would make a good torturer. Which led her to wonder what sort of information she could want so badly that it would make her deliberately hurt someone.

Then she knew.

"Where is the key to the library?"

As soon as she thought of it, she started to laugh. She had to cough to cover up the fact that she was laughing.

But even for the library key, she didn't think she could hurt anybody directly. So how could she torture someone without actually hurting them? Thinking of ideas and rejecting them took up a long chunk of time.

Then she hit upon the perfect torture, at least for herself. Watching her sister, Nooria, brush her long, thick hair. That always drove Parvana crazy, and Nooria knew it, so she always seemed to wait until Parvana was around to start brushing. Even when Parvana grew her hair long, it was straggly and wispy and didn't behave. Nooria had the most beautiful hair Parvana had ever seen. When Nooria was younger, she enjoyed flipping it in Parvana's face, taunting her with it.

She hasn't changed much, Parvana thought, as she nodded off to sleep again.

As soon as her chin touched her chest, the baseball bat banged against the metal wall by her head. She jolted awake, wishing she could break that bat into a million pieces.

They probably have more bats, she thought. They probably have a whole shed full of baseball bats that they use to keep people awake.

To keep herself from slipping into sleep again, Parvana decided to think about Nooria, and the day the letters came.

TEN

The first letter came in the morning.

The school was in the middle of Dust Duty.

Dust Duty was the chore that involved getting the dust and sand out of the school. A never-ending chore, since the school was on the edge of a desert. Some girls were sweeping out classrooms and hallways. Others were sliding rags over windowsills and tables.

Parvana had what she thought was the best chore — beating carpets. She would fling a rug over a clothesline and beat it with a stick. Clouds of dust and dirt filled the air. A fair bit of it landed on Parvana. She sneezed, laughed and shook it out of her hair.

She spied Maryam off by herself, making up some kind of dance steps when she was supposed to be cleaning.

"This is Dust Duty, not Dance Duty," Parvana told her.

"All the rags are taken," Maryam said, doing some fancy little twists with her hands.

"There's also something called a broom."

"All the brooms are taken, too."

"All of them?" Parvana took hold of her sister's dancing hand and led her around the corner of the school. "I am sure we can find at least one broom tucked away in the storage shed."

The shed was against the back wall of the school yard. It held everything from a box of donated sandals to garden tools.

Parvana reached for the shed door. Then she noticed the padlock.

"Since when is this shed locked?" she asked. "Who put this here?"

"Mr. Fahir put it on," Maryam said. "I told you there were no more brooms."

"Go and ask Mr. Fahir to come here and bring the key," Parvana told her.

"Ask him yourself," Maryam replied. And she danced away.

Parvana saw Mr. Fahir crossing the yard and ran over to him.

"Mr. Fahir, do you have the key for the storage shed? My sister needs a broom."

"Broom?" Mr. Fahir asked. "I don't think we have any more brooms in the shed."

"Well, she needs something to keep her busy. And why are we locking the shed?"

"The shed should be locked," he replied. "Children should not go in there."

"The students don't go in," Parvana said. "It's always unlocked and there's never been a problem — "

"A letter has come," he said, interrupting her. "I was just taking it in."

He held up a large brown envelope.

Mail service had finally returned to Afghanistan after years of war, but it wasn't common for people to get letters. Certainly Parvana had never received one. She had written plenty of letters to Shauzia over the years, but she had never mailed them. She had no idea where Shauzia was, so the letters stayed in her father's old shoulder bag.

"It's from America," Mr. Fahir told her.

"Who is it for?" she asked. "Is it for me?"

She allowed herself one fleeting moment of fantasy about the letter being from Shauzia, saying she had left the lavender field in France and was now sitting in a corn field in America.

Mr. Fahir handed her the envelope.

It was for Nooria.

"If you will take it inside, I will find something for your little sister to do," he said.

Parvana stared at the envelope as she walked.

Why would Nooria get a letter from America? Parvana was tempted to rip it open. It took every ounce of self-control to keep the envelope sealed all the way to Nooria's classroom.

Nooria was supervising her students on Dust Duty there.

Parvana tapped her on the arm. "This came for you."

"I'm in the middle of something."

"Never mind, then," Parvana said. "I'll toss your letter from America on the cook fire."

Nooria took the envelope from her and looked at it.

"It came," she said.

"What is it?"

"Is Mother in her office?"

"How should I — "

But Nooria didn't wait for an answer. She dashed from the classroom, taking the envelope with her.

Parvana was stuck supervising Nooria's class until the bell rang for recess. Then she hurried off to find her sister.

Nooria was in their mother's office. They were deep in conversation. The envelope was open, its contents spread across the desk.

They didn't even look up when Parvana walked in.

"What is it?" she asked. "What's in the letter?"

Nooria looked up. Parvana saw a joy and excitement on her sister's face that she couldn't remember seeing ever before.

"It's from New York University," she said, jumping up and giving Parvana a hug — very un-Nooria-like. She practically squealed. "I've been accepted to their school! They will pay for everything! I'm going to America!"

America! Parvana couldn't believe it. She broke off from her sister and snatched up the letter.

There it was, in clear type. *We are pleased to tell you that you have been accepted to the Visiting Scholar Program at New York University, on full scholarship.*

Nooria grabbed the letter before Parvana could finish reading it. Parvana didn't care.

They were going to America! And not just America — New York. Central Park, the Empire State Building, the Statue of Liberty and brand new things to see on streets she had never walked before.

"When do we go?" she asked. "I can be ready in an hour. Half an hour. I can be ready in two minutes!" Really, all she needed was her father's shoulder bag. She owned nothing else that she cared about. In a city that big there would be jobs she could do that would help her earn money to buy the things she needed.

"Will we live near the subway?" she asked. What a wonderful thing it would be to live near a subway ...

Then she realized that Mother and Nooria were looking at her — Nooria with scorn and amusement, Mother with a combination of pity and exasperation.

"You're not going anywhere," Nooria said, holding the letter right up to Parvana's face. "It's my name on the paper. I'm going."

"Take me with you," Parvana said, not caring that

she was begging. "Why should you get to go and I have to stay? And how did they find out about you? What have you done that's so special?"

Parvana knew she was acting like a four-year-old child, but she couldn't stop herself. She swatted away the letter, wishing she dared swat Nooria's taunting face.

"Mother and I applied. And I got accepted because of how I suffered in the war."

"How you suffered? All you ever did was wash your hair — over and over and over. I know because I had to go out and fetch the water!"

"Girls! That's enough!" Mother got up from her chair and closed the office door.

That won't do any good, Parvana thought. These walls are thin.

She was so angry she didn't care who heard.

"We sent in the application months ago," Mother said. "We had no idea that she would be accepted, and now that she has been, we are very happy."

"Why didn't you apply for me, too?"

"You're too young, and you haven't gone far enough in school," Mother said firmly. "Now, stop this nonsense and tell your sister you're happy."

Parvana was working hard to get to a place in her head where she could be happy for her sister, when Nooria chimed in.

"Besides, you can't even multiply fractions."

That set Parvana off again.

"I can so!" She could, too. By now she could multiply them, divide them and turn them into decimals. And Nooria knew it.

"Nooria will come back to Afghanistan as an educated woman," Mother said. "She'll be able to take over the school one day."

"And then you'll be working for me!" Nooria smirked the nastiest smirk Parvana had ever seen. Nastier than the smirks of Hanifa and Sharifa combined.

"I will never work for you! Never!" Parvana's fists were clenched so tight she could feel her nails puncturing the skin on her palms.

"I think the thing that swayed the university to give me the scholarship was the part where I told them I dressed up as a boy during the Taliban and went out to work to feed my family," Nooria told her.

Mother intercepted Parvana as she lunged at her sister. And then Parvana found herself firmly on the other side of the locked office door.

"That's *my* life!" Parvana said, banging and kicking. "You stole *my* life!"

Parvana ran outside, past a sea of students who had gathered to watch the fun.

She went back to her carpet-beating station and attacked the carpet with fury. At one point she swung her stick so hard that it flew up over the wall of the school and fell on the other side.

Parvana hoped the stick had landed on someone's head. She had a deep need to hurt somebody.

What happened, though, was that she still had carpets to clean. She had to leave the grounds, walk around the school wall and retrieve the stick. By the time she did that, her rage was gone, and she was too empty to feel anything.

The second letter came in the night.

Parvana was in the yard to witness its arrival, too.

She hadn't gone to class or supper and she certainly wasn't about to go to bed on the toshak between the awful Nooria and the not-awful Maryam who was annoyingly making a long list of presents she wanted Nooria to buy for her in New York.

Mother let her be. Everyone stayed away.

Everyone except Asif. He brought her a plate of nan and chickpeas and a mug of tea, and he wrapped a blanket around her shoulders.

"I never liked Nooria," was all he said. It was enough.

Parvana ate, then made a little bed for herself against the Leila's Academy of Hope sign.

It was good to be sleeping under the stars again. She knew how to sleep on the ground. A mattress was nice, but it wasn't necessary. As long as she had a blanket.

She thought again about just walking away.

She could become the Wild Girl of Afghanistan. People would see her and then in a flash she'd be gone. Legends would spring up.

"The Wild Girl was here last night," they would say. "One of Naseer's chickens is missing."

"The Wild Girl drew water from our well. We will have good luck this year!"

Years would go by. She would become the Wild Woman of Afghanistan, then the Wild Old Woman. She would live to be a very old woman because she would get lots of fresh air and exercise and would never get married. She would be her own boss all her life. And she would be happy.

Parvana was just starting to picture her death on the top of a hill right beneath a rising full moon, at the age of one hundred and one, when she heard the sound of a car engine.

It stopped close to the school. A car door opened and then something came flying over the school wall. It landed in the yard near Parvana's feet. The car door closed and the car sped away.

It was all over before Parvana could react and call Mr. Fahir, who was sleeping in his little room by the gate.

She looked at the object that had been thrown.

It was a rock about the size of a brick.

A piece of paper was bound to it with string.

Parvana picked it up, pulled off the string and un-folded the paper. It was too dark outside to see, so she went inside to the kitchen. She took a box of matches out of the drawer, struck one and held it up to the paper.

Close down your school, it said, *or you will pay the price. Close down your school or we will kill you.*

Parvana read the words over and over until the flame hit her fingertips and she blew out the match.

All at once, and at long last, she was glad her sister was getting out.

ELEVEN

"*Dear Shauzia: It is getting harder and harder to remember what you look like ...*"

Parvana stood and listened to the interpreter read the words she had written to her friend so long ago. She had written the letters in Dari. They sounded strange as they came out of the corporal's mouth in English for the major's benefit.

"*... My life is dust and rocks and rude boys and skinny babies, and long days searching for my mother when I don't have the faintest idea where she might be.*"

"Whoever wrote that sounds very sad," the major said. "What do you think, Corporal? Think this Shauzia is an actual person?"

"The notebook could just be a diary, sir," the woman replied. "Many girls give their diaries names. Anne Frank called hers Kitty."

"I read my older sister's diary when we were kids," the major said. "Dull reading. All about how she hated her hair and hated her legs and hated her nose and was sure no one would ever like her. I never teased her about it, though. I didn't want her to know that I knew she felt so bad about herself. It was more information about her than I wanted to know."

"I understand, sir."

"Read on, Corporal."

The interpreter read from letter to letter. Parvana was too fed up even to be angry at this invasion of her privacy.

"Dear Shauzia: We are back on the road. It almost feels like we never left. Maybe Green Valley was just a dream. I should stop dreaming. All my dreams turn to garbage ..."

"'Dreams turn to garbage,'" the major quoted. "People become disillusioned, they can easily turn to violence. We've seen that before, haven't we, Corporal?"

"Yes, sir."

She turned a page and kept reading.

"Dear Shauzia: Someone in this camp has a radio and I heard that the Taliban are gone and there is a new government in Kabul. The news is causing

a lot of arguments. Some say things will get better. Others say things will get worse. Some say the foreign troops will kill all the Afghans and move into their homes. When one man heard that, he waved his arms in front of his tent made from trash bags and said, 'They want my house? They can have it.' Rumors are spreading faster than dysentery. No one knows what is happening. But I know. I know that whatever those important people are doing in Kabul, they are not thinking about girls like me, or about any of us who are lost and living in the mud."

More pages turned.

"Dear Shauzia: I hate the foreign military. In the newspaper today there was a story about a foreign missile hitting a village and killing a bunch of children. And yesterday, a soldier was in Mother's office. Of course, I listened at the door. He wanted Mother to give him information on all our staff. Mother told him that her job was running a school, not spying for the army. She said she personally knew all of her staff and that nothing would make them less safe than their neighbors seeing the military come to their homes. She said the army should spend more time going after the people who are blowing up schools and killing teachers and less time bothering innocent people. Then she kicked him out so fast I nearly got hit by the office door. Mother was so angry at him that

she took it out on me with a long list of extra chores — another reason for me to hate the foreigners!"

"Sounds to me like there's quite a bit of anger there, Corporal. Enough to make her a terrorist? I guess that's what we're here to find out."

Parvana had to stand and listen to her life being spouted back at her, and she had to pretend that she didn't understand a word.

TWELVE

"How do I know it works?"

Parvana stood beside her mother and Asif in the small tailor shop. The tailor pulled the chair away from the table and made a gesture, inviting Mother to sit down and try the sewing machine out herself.

Parvana laughed. Her mother had been a professional journalist before the Taliban came, and now she was the headmistress of a school. She could do many things, but she could not operate a sewing machine.

Mother frowned and nodded at Asif. He had also never used a sewing machine, but he could figure out how it worked within a minute of sitting down in front of it.

"No electricity required," the tailor said. "It operates by pedal. Just move your foot."

Asif shifted in his seat so that his foot was on the middle of the pedal. Parvana watched him stitch a seam. It looked pretty straight to her.

"There is a gear that seems to be sticking," Asif said.

"A drop of oil, it will work like new."

"We'll see," Asif replied. "Where are the others?"

The tailor took Asif to the back to show him the other machines. The school was going to set up a sewing class.

"He'll be a while," Mother said. "Let's look at fabric."

They headed off through the market. The fabric alley was draped with colors and textures from the cloth that hung down like branches. Mother picked a stall with a wide choice of fabric and started a long discussion with the owner. Every now and then Parvana would offer a suggestion or point to something she liked, but Mother ignored her. She had plenty of her own ideas.

The school's first year was over, and the new year was about to begin. Nooria had gone to New York, and she had been very nice to Parvana for nearly all of her last three weeks in Afghanistan.

After she left, Mother cried for four days. Then she got very busy and insisted everyone else be busy, too. When Parvana, Maryam and Asif were not cleaning, painting and getting the school ready to start up again, they were working in the vegetable garden. They also studied every night.

Now that she had mastered the art of multiplying fractions, Parvana did not mind the lessons. She worked hard and steadily, passing through the sixth- and seventh-class workbooks and starting on the eighth.

"If you keep this up, you'll be in high school

soon," Mother told her. "You're quickly catching up to your age level."

Parvana had a new, secret plan to get a scholarship to the Sorbonne in Paris. She would find Shauzia and become richer and more successful than Nooria.

Nooria would say, "You must come and visit me in New York City. I can see the Statue of Liberty from my apartment window."

And Parvana would reply, "The Statue of Liberty is very nice. In Paris, we have the Eiffel Tower. And, by the way, I own it! I bought it! That's right. I designed a house that fits right inside and now I live there."

Parvana found that to be such an exciting idea that she put her hand in her pocket and took out the pen and paper she always carried with her now. She had so many ideas that she couldn't trust them to stay in her head. She wrote them down right away so they couldn't escape.

She drew a sketch of the Eiffel Tower, then put a house right in the middle of it. It could have different levels, she thought, like a treehouse, and big windows on all sides so she could see who was out on the grounds. And she would hang big banners on each side saying *Parvana's House* and *Welcome Shauzia*.

She was adding a giant swing when Mother bumped into her, reaching for a bolt of green cotton.

Parvana dropped her pen.

"You could try to be helpful instead of just standing there," her mother said. It was an automatic

Mother comment that meant nothing. Her mother did not want her help buying fabric. Her mother just wanted her to carry the fabric after she bought it.

Parvana tried to spot her pen.

She had heard it drop, but it wasn't at her feet.

She stared at the ground until she spotted it right under the fabric merchant's feet.

I can't ask him for it, she thought. He looks exasperated enough already.

Mother was not an easy customer.

She waited until Mother asked to see something on the top shelf. He moved his foot, freeing the pen, but then he accidentally kicked it away as he reached for the ladder. The pen rolled down the alley.

Parvana went after it.

As soon as it stopped, it was kicked away by another foot. It rolled and rolled through the market.

Parvana was sure she looked ridiculous — a full-grown girl chasing after a pen.

Finally, the pen came to a stop against the wall of a bedding and blanket shop. Parvana bent down and scooped it up.

As she stood up, her heart stopped.

There was a notice pasted on the wall. Its words were big, clear and angry.

To the parents who send their daughters to the Leila School:
This school is run by evil people. If you let

your daughters go, then you are evil, too.
Evil must be destroyed. You have been
warned.

Parvana stared and stared. She couldn't move.
"There you are!"
Mother came up behind her, arms full of parcels.
"Help me with these. Really, you are more trouble than Hassan and Maryam put together. If I can't trust you not to wander — "
Then Mother spotted the notice. And she stopped talking.
Parvana crammed the pen into her pocket and attacked the notice. It was stuck to the wall with glue and would not rip off, no matter how much she scraped at it with her fingernails.
"Parvana, come ..." Mother tried to pull her away.
Parvana took out her pen and tried to stab the notice out of existence, and when that didn't work, she started to scribble all over it.
"Parvana. Come!"
Mother grabbed her firmly by the arm and pulled, hard.
Only then did Parvana realize she had drawn a crowd. A half-circle of men surrounded Parvana and her mother.
Parvana had learned from her last mistake. This time she did not run. Instead, she looked each man in the face.

"The Prophet Muhammad, peace be upon him, says in the Holy Qur'an that all are called to be educated, women and men alike. If you worry about what goes on in our school, come and see it for yourself. You know where we are. Knock at the gate. Ask for me. My name is Parvana. I will give you a tour."

Her fingers found a loose edge on the notice. She grabbed hold of it and pulled. It ripped clean through. Now nobody could read the awful message.

"Here, Mother, let me help you carry those," Parvana said, taking some of the parcels of fabric. Then she put her hand through her mother's arm and they started walking. She could feel her mother trembling and remembered that while she was used to being outside in the marketplace, her mother was not.

The men let them move through.

Walking away, Parvana was filled with a sense of triumph. Those men would talk about her now. They would talk about what she had said, and then they would add, "That brave girl is right! Education is the duty of everyone!"

Father used to call me his little Malali, Parvana thought.

Malali was a girl in Afghan history, famous for leading troops into battle against the British. And now Parvana was doing the same, rallying people not to war, but to education.

She straightened her back and raised her head higher.

That's when she saw the other notices.

They were everywhere — on walls, pasted on signs, nailed onto poles. Everywhere Parvana looked, she saw the warning notices. She was walking through a forest of hatred.

I'll have to burn down the market to get rid of them all, she thought.

Her confidence and celebration drained right out of her. Asif was ready and waiting at the tailor's with a taxi to take them and the sewing machines back to the school.

He took one look at her face and got them out of there quickly.

For once, Parvana felt grateful when the high walls of the school compound wrapped around them, keeping out the rest of the world.

THIRTEEN

Parvana was back in the little office, standing again, the same guard staring at her.

She was having a hard day. She was so tired! She was even too tired to summon any thoughts to distract herself.

They kept changing her routine. She never knew what was going on or what was going to happen next. That made it impossible for her to relax.

They kept thinking up new things to do to her. They would not let her sleep.

The latest thing was music. They piped music into her cell. Loud music. The same song over and over and over. Some young man singing about puppy love. As soon as he finished singing his song, he started again from the beginning.

Parvana had no quiet, no place in her brain to gather her thoughts. Only puppy love, puppy love, puppy love, hour after hour.

I might just go crazy, Parvana thought. No matter how hard I try not to. I'll be like the woman on the hill I passed by all those years ago. All she did was sit and wail, far away from everybody.

Parvana wondered if the woman was still there. Maybe Parvana could sit and wail on the next hill over. They could sort of keep each other company.

The questioning man and interpreting woman entered the office then.

"You can go," the man said to the soldier, who saluted and disappeared.

They both had paper cups of coffee and they each carried a book. The man also carried an open box of donuts that he placed on the desk. They took their seats, opened their books and began to read.

The sight of books caused such excitement to stir in Parvana that she could barely contain herself. It was all she could do not to cross the office, take their books away, plop herself down on the floor and start reading herself.

To calm herself, she concentrated on the donuts.

There were six in the box. Two were covered in white powdered sugar. Two were chocolate, with chocolate icing. Two had pink icing with colored sprinkles.

Parvana tried to guess who would eat which donut first, and was delighted when she guessed right. The woman took a chocolate donut, the man took one with the powdered sugar. It squirted a blob of red jelly onto his boot. He didn't notice.

She did some mental arithmetic — fractions and percentages, based on the donuts left in the box — while the soldiers took the lids off their coffees, opened their books and settled in to read.

Only then did Parvana take a look at what they were reading.

The man was reading *The Constant Gardener* by John le Carré.

Parvana had never heard of it, but she liked the title. She would like to be a constant gardener. All day long, she would dig and plant and water and harvest.

It seemed an odd choice of book for a man who spent all his time barking questions at a teenaged girl.

Maybe he would rather be a gardener, too.

Then she looked at what the woman was reading. It was *Jane Eyre* by Charlotte Brontë.

Parvana hadn't read that book, either, and the title gave no clues as to what it was about.

Her captors sat and read, drank their coffee and ignored Parvana.

Parvana didn't care. She was so grateful for the silence! She wanted to put all the silence in a big sack and carry it with her. And she was grateful for the idea of becoming a constant gardener. She got lost in thoughts of what sort of a garden she would have if she didn't have to do anything else. Planning a garden was like planning a village. It had to be useable but should also look and feel good. Parvana's mind became full of pathways and benches, tomato plants and big heads of cauliflower.

When the paper cups were drained of coffee and

only crumbs and stray sprinkles remained in the box, the man and woman put down their books and started in again on Parvana.

"Are you tired of my jail yet?" the man asked, while the woman translated. "Perhaps this is paradise for you. You have a bed to sleep in. An indoor latrine. Food every day. Is that why you're not talking, so you can keep living in my jail?"

He paused, as if he really expected her to answer. Then he continued.

"If that's what you're thinking, you'd better think again. We are in the Peace Business, not in the business of giving nice homes to little girls who are too stubborn to talk to us. We're not going to put up with this much longer. Right now you have a nice private cell all to yourself. You get the same food we get, which is pretty darn good, and you have your own latrine! I don't have my own latrine. I have to share with the other officers, and some of those guys are slobs.

"You are also currently enjoying, piped right into your cell, the musical stylings of one Donny Osmond. But don't think you're going to stay in this lap of luxury forever. When our generosity runs out, your time here is done.

"There are much worse places than this, and much worse people than us. We don't want to turn you over to them, but we may not have any choice. If we are not one hundred percent certain that you are not a threat, we will make sure that you are locked up forever. You have to prove to us that we can trust you. And you can start by talking. Or screaming. Or crying. Give us some sign that we are getting through to you."

The man talked on and on, with the woman translating. To Parvana's ears, it all became just a different version of the dog song.

Her head hurt.

"We are going over the ruins of that school with a fine-toothed comb. We are compiling evidence against you, charges you will have to answer for. Maybe you're innocent. Maybe you were just there by accident, just in the wrong place at the wrong time. We don't think so. After all, we are not in the habit of locking up people who haven't done anything wrong. But maybe in your case we made a mistake.

"Right now, it looks like you are involved in some very bad activities, activities that are disgraceful for a young girl. I don't want to believe it! I know you think I'm mean and heartless, but I truly want you to be innocent. But I need proof. I'm not the boss here. I have people to answer to. And those people are saying things to me, things that I'd be worried about if I were you."

He stopped talking for a bit, as if to let his words sink in.

"You need to appreciate the sort of pressure I am

under. This can't go on indefinitely. It has to come to an end, soon, one way or another."

He took another pause.

"I have money at my disposal," he said unexpectedly. "The taxpayers of my country have sent money over here for two things: punish evil-doers and reward good-doers. Which one are you? Talk to me. One word. Show us you are a good-doer and I will release you with enough money in your pocket to have a very nice life. More money than you have ever seen. You could go to school, buy yourself nice clothes, start a business. Whatever you want to do. Under the right circumstances, I can be a very generous — "

An explosion cut into his words.

Somewhere on the base, not far from the office, something was blowing up.

The room shook and filled with a roar of dynamite crashing through concrete. The major and the corporal were thrown from their chairs and Parvana was knocked to the floor. The sound was deafening. Sirens followed. Running boots filled the hallway.

Parvana sat up, curling her arms around her knees and keeping her head low, but not so low that she couldn't see what was happening.

The man and woman were back on their feet. They stood in the doorway a moment, looking out. There was yelling and screaming, orders being shouted and names being called out.

And then the miracle happened.

Parvana was left alone.

Maybe they've forgotten about me, she thought.

She didn't wait around to give them a chance to remember.

In a flash, she was on her feet and at the office door. She looked out into the hall. Everyone was running in every direction. Parvana could smell smoke and gasoline.

Someone or something had attacked the base.

It had nothing to do with Parvana. She grabbed the closest book — *Jane Eyre* — tucked it into her clothes and slipped into the hallway. If she could just get outside, maybe she could keep going.

Just inside the door to the outside world was a desk that usually had a guard sitting at it. The guard wasn't there. He was running around dealing with the emergency. But he had left behind his pen.

Parvana snatched it up and made it disappear into her pants pocket. Then she headed outside.

She stepped out into chaos.

The attack had been a bad one. Parvana didn't know if it was a rocket or a suicide bomber or even one of the army's own bombs that had taken a wrong turn somewhere.

It didn't matter. Fires were burning. People were screaming. Soldiers shouted orders and ran around with stretchers to fetch the wounded.

No one noticed Parvana.

The explosion had blown a hole in the fence. She walked closer. She could see the fields ahead, opening to her like welcoming arms.

She knew how to live in her country. If she could get beyond the wire, she could keep going. She could run up into the hills and disappear forever.

She broke into a run. One more person running would not be noticed. She was dressed in army-green. No one gave her a second glance.

She ran for all she was worth, shedding her exhaustion and leaving it behind in the dust. Her bare feet slapped hard against the gravel and sand. She could sleep in the hills. She could collapse on the good, rocky, nothing-will-grow-here soil and sleep under the Afghan moon and stars.

All she needed to do was to keep running ...

"Help me!"

The voice was weak and full of pain. Parvana heard it through the noise, even though she told herself she didn't.

In spite of telling herself sternly not to look for the source of it, she looked.

A young soldier, a woman, was pinned under some rubble and razor wire. Blood gushed from an artery in her neck. The soldier's arms were pinned down by blocks of concrete, and she could not help herself.

Parvana looked around.

One of the other soldiers would notice this woman and help her. They would get to her in time. She would be sent to a fancy hospital and sent home, all fixed and healthy.

Surely someone else would get to her before it was too late.

Parvana ran a few steps more. The gap in the fence was within reach. Thirty seconds of hard running and she would be through.

Thirty seconds. A lot of blood could empty out of a human body in thirty seconds.

She had no choice.

She turned around, taking off her long-sleeved shirt while she ran. She knelt by the terrified soldier and pressed the rolled-up shirt against the woman's neck.

"I need help!" Parvana yelled in English. She waved her free arm. "Medic!"

It seemed like an eternity of pressing on the wound and waving and yelling and, in between, telling the woman not to worry, that she would be all right.

When the medic arrived, he gave directions to Parvana and she followed each one.

They had drilled for this in first-aid class. She knew what to do.

The stretcher-bearers finally got there. Parvana backed away. She started to run again.

She made it to the fence. She ran through the gap and planned to keep on running, right across the plain and right up into the hills.

"Hands in the air!"

An armored car zoomed to a stop right in front of her. Machine guns pointed at her.

"Down on your knees, or I will shoot you!"

The soldiers, in full battle gear, with helmets instead of faces, blocked Parvana's view of the mountains.

For a long moment, she thought she would just keep on running.

After all, at this point, she had nothing left to lose.

But she didn't. She raised her arms, dropped to her knees and hoped they would at least let her keep the pen.

FOURTEEN

The warning posters worked. When the new school year began, student enrollment was down.

"But it is still a great day," Mother said on the first day of term. "We are still here. That's what matters. That's a victory."

They had a first-day assembly. Mother gave a terrific speech, telling everyone to work hard and do their best for Afghanistan. It was a short assembly. Mother believed in setting the tone the first day by getting everyone right to work.

Parvana felt surprisingly happy as she headed to the dining hall with her books. She had studied hard during the break. She had trained her body to be able to sit for a long time and she had trained her mind to focus. The return of the students meant more work in a lot of ways, but it also meant more hands to do the work.

"Parvana, come here a moment."

Mother waved her over after the assembly.

"I need you to take over a class," she said. "The

teacher I hired to replace Nooria hasn't shown up. I'm trying to track her down, but I need you to watch the girls in the meantime."

"What do I do?"

"Teach them something!"

Mother hurried away. Parvana headed to what had been Nooria's classroom. Twenty girls waited for her there.

"Where's our teacher?" one of them asked.

"The headmistress is trying to find out. I'm just filling in."

Two girls stood up and headed for the door.

"Who are you and where are you going?" Parvana asked them.

"I'm Farah and this is my sister. We're supposed to go home if there isn't a real teacher."

"Why would anyone tell you that?"

"Our parents told us that the teachers have been warned to stay away. They said if we had no teacher we should come home, or people will say we are here doing bad things."

"Go back to your desks," Parvana ordered.

"But …"

"I said go back to your desks." Parvana squared her shoulders. "Your teacher is here."

When the sisters were in their seats, Parvana said sharply, "Class stand."

The girls all stood, but they rose clumsily, slowly and shyly. Parvana wasn't satisfied.

"Try again," Parvana said. "This time, everyone stand on the left side of your desk."

Not all the girls knew their left side from their right, so they had to get that sorted out.

They tried again.

"Class stand."

Parvana took them through it a few times.

"Better," she told them. "I want you to do that whenever I or another teacher enters your classroom. It is a sign of respect."

It was also one of the things she remembered from when she had attended school many years before.

"Now let's see how much arithmetic you know."

Parvana worked them hard. The morning session passed quickly in a haze of quizzes, games and reading out loud. By lunch time she was drained but excited.

"The morning went really well," she told her mother. "They were answering questions. They were learning! And I think they had fun."

"Did you take attendance?" Mother asked.

Parvana hadn't even thought of that. "I'll do it after lunch."

"Our funders need to know how many students we have each day. If our numbers fall much more, we won't get as much money from the aid agencies. They'll think we aren't doing our job. So that attendance record is important. Ask one of the other teachers to help you. They'll get you set up."

"You mean I'll be keeping the class?"

"Until I get a real teacher to replace you. I'll teach your students myself when I can, but I can't be in the classroom every day. I know this will be a lot of work for you. You'll have to do your own school work in the evenings. I hope it won't be for long. You've made such progress."

"One of my students told me the villagers are saying that the teachers have been threatened." Parvana liked saying "my students."

Mother rubbed her eyes. She looked very tired and it was only the middle of the day.

"Go and get your lunch, Parvana, then get back to your class. I'll try to spend some time with you tonight. We'll make up some lesson plans."

Parvana went to the dining hall. She got her tray of food and headed toward a table of students, then changed her mind. She took her tray to the teachers' table.

Before she went back to her class she slipped into her family's sleeping quarters. She took off the white chador that all the students wore and put on a dark blue one that Nooria had left behind.

She looked at herself in the mirror. She looked fine.

Even if Mother hired another teacher, she would never go back to being an ordinary student.

"I was born to be in charge," she said to her reflection.

Then she hurried off to her classroom.

After all, lunch was over. Her students were waiting.

FIFTEEN

A couple of months into the term, Parvana pushed back the bolt on the school's metal gate very early one morning. She wanted to see if the newspaper had arrived. She liked to start each day talking with her class about what was going on in the world.

Asif usually got to the newspaper first, and then he was insufferable. By the time Parvana arrived in the dining hall for her breakfast nan and tea, he already had all the news.

He enjoyed lording it over her, too.

"What do you think will happen at the president's conference today?" he'd ask her, knowing she didn't know what the conference was all about. Or, "Can you believe what happened in Italy?"

Then Parvana would have to ask, "What conference?" or "What happened in Italy?"

Today, though, *she* would get the news first, and she would be the one to announce it all at breakfast.

The newspaper was there, tossed into the weeds by the side of the driveway. Parvana picked it up and started to unroll it.

As she headed back into the school yard, she spotted something else on the ground.

At first it looked like a big sack tied up with a rope. Then she saw the small feet sticking out of it.

"Mr. Fahir!" she called out.

She dropped the newspaper and ran to the bundle, untying the rope and flinging away the rags that covered it.

The child moved. It was alive.

Parvana gently brushed the hair away from the child's face.

A little girl stared back at her.

"Salaam alaikum," Parvana said. "Who are you?"

The child whimpered.

Parvana's calls had awakened her mother.

"What's going on?"

"Somebody dropped off their daughter," Mr. Fahir said. "It happened in the night. I didn't see or hear anything."

"They tied her up and left her!" said Parvana.

Mr. Fahir scooped up the girl in his arms. They all went into the dining hall where the woodstove was newly lit and giving off some warmth. Away from the cool morning air, they could smell how filthy the girl was.

"She weighs nothing," said Mr. Fahir. He slowly put her down on a chair.

"What's your name?" Mother asked her. "Who left you out there? Where are you from?"

The little girl didn't answer.

"Her name is Ava," Parvana said. "Look."

A note was pinned to the child's rags. It was written with crudely made letters.

Name Ava
       Father dead   Mother dead
Good girl

"She's an orphan," Parvana said.

"There's something wrong with her," Mother said.

There was something different about Ava. Her eyes didn't quite focus and her mouth didn't quite close.

"How old are you, Ava?" Mother asked.

Ava didn't reply. She was too busy looking at Parvana.

"Do you know how old you are?" Parvana knelt down close to the girl and smiled when she asked.

Ava made grunting sounds and touched Parvana's face with her fingers.

"I'll have to make some calls," Mother said. "This is a school, not a hospital. We're not equipped to take care of her. I do not need this today." She headed to her office.

"I'll heat some water," Mr. Fahir said. He put his hand on Ava's head. "She could probably use a bath." He smiled at Parvana and got to work.

Parvana got Ava a drink of water and a small piece

of bread. She didn't know when Ava had last eaten, but she knew that eating a lot when you haven't eaten anything for a long time was not good for you. Ava chewed on the bread.

When the water was hot, Parvana took the kettle and Ava into the family's quarters to get her cleaned up.

"Get her away from me," Maryam said, as she tried out hairstyles in front of a small mirror. "She smells."

"So do you sometimes. Get me your old shalwar kameez."

"No," Maryam said. "It's mine. I don't want it on that ugly girl."

Parvana took Maryam by the shoulders. "Her name is Ava, and you speak to her nicely. As hard as your life has been, hers has been ten times harder. Get me your old shalwar kameez or I'll give Ava your new one."

"I hate you!" Maryam said, flinging the shalwar kameez at her. "I wish Nooria was here and you were in New York!" She stomped out of the room.

"She's a very nice girl when she's asleep," Parvana said to Ava with a smile. "Let's get you clean."

The rags fell apart as Parvana removed them. They were rotten, filthy and beyond saving.

As the dirt on the child's skin was washed away, Parvana made a terrible discovery.

There were scars on the little girl's body — round

burn marks from cigarettes being put out on her skin, scars in the shape of barbed wire around her wrists and ankles.

"Somebody hurt you," Parvana whispered.

The scars were old, not fresh, but Parvana was still extra gentle as she rubbed a soapy washcloth over Ava's skin.

She slowly poured water over the girl's head and worked the soap into a lather. Ava whimpered, but she let herself be washed.

When Ava was clean and dry and dressed in clean clothes, Parvana tried to comb her hair. It was hopelessly matted.

"I'm going to have to cut your hair," she said, "but it will look pretty. I promise."

She fetched some scissors and gave her as long a cut as she could. She managed to turn the tangled mess into a style that curled naturally around Ava's ears and neck.

"We'll go to the market and get you a hair ribbon," she said. Then she took the child in to see Mother.

"She's all clean," Parvana said.

Mother put down her cell phone. "She looks like a different girl. Now we can see your beautiful face," she said to Ava.

"I told her we'd get her a hair ribbon."

"A hair ribbon is easy. A home is harder. I haven't found anyone who will take her."

"I think we should keep her."

"She's not a stray puppy, Parvana. She's a human being, one we are not able to look after."

Parvana brought Ava around the desk and stood her in front of her mother.

"Someone hurt her," Parvana said. "Look."

Mother looked, touched the scars and slipped her arm around Ava's shoulders.

"Well, we're not going to shove her back out the gate. We'll keep her here, but only until we find someplace better."

"There is no place better," Parvana said.

She took Ava's hand and they went back to the dining hall for hot tea and a real breakfast.

Asif was reading the newspaper first.

Parvana didn't care.

Her news was bigger than his.

SIXTEEN

E xcept for freedom, Parvana had, for the moment, everything she needed.

She was back in her old cell. For warmth, she had a blanket. She draped it over her shoulders and head so that it hung down over her lap. It covered her face, it covered the bloodstained T-shirt she still wore two days after the explosion, and it covered the copy of *Jane Eyre*, open on her crossed legs.

No new meals had come since the attack, but she had been careful to save her leftovers from the meals that came before. On the little shelf above her table she had a package of nuts, a peanut butter and jam sandwich, cheese and crackers and something called SpaghettiOs — all in their own foil packets.

Tucked away under her mattress were several pieces of paper, taken out of the meal bags, and one lovely working pen. She hadn't done anything but test it out to make sure it still had ink, but that was enough. She knew it was there.

She was tucked up on the cot, a chocolate brownie in her hand and Charlotte Brontë's book on her lap.

She nibbled on the brownie, lost herself in Jane, Mr.
Rochester and the mad woman in the attic of Thorn-
field Hall.

At first she thought she would just read a chapter
to make it last, but she decided not to bother ration-
ing it. At any minute of any day, soldiers could come
into her room and take everything away. They could
move her to another jail. They could take her out
into the desert, shoot her and leave her body for the
buzzards.

She decided to devour the book. The more she
read, the more she would have in her mind to enter-
tain herself the next time they made her stand in that
horrible little office.

The other wonderful thing Parvana had now was
silence — blessed, beautiful silence. Donny Osmond
had finally stopped singing. He seemed to have been
wounded in the blast. Every now and then his song
would squeak on again. It would whine and wheeze
for a few bars and then sputter out and die.

She forgot about Mr. Osmond and got back to
Jane Eyre.

Jane had just run away from the still-married Mr.
Rochester and was in the strange village begging for
bread, when Parvana heard a weird noise.

Into the quiet cell came the sound of someone
crying.

The sobbing was muffled, as if the crier was trying
to not let anyone know he was crying.

It sounded like it was coming from outside Parvana's window.

Parvana put down her book, shucked the blanket and balanced herself on the cot and the table. She pressed her face against the shutters.

A man was sitting underneath her window. He was crying.

It's a good place to cry, Parvana thought.

It was private, or as private as it was possible to get. She didn't imagine it would be good for a soldier's image to be found sobbing. Even the women had to act tough.

Parvana listened to the crying for a while.

Was the man homesick? Did he lose a friend in the explosion? Had someone hurt him? Was he lonely?

Parvana thought about calling down to him, but she couldn't think of anything to say.

Then she thought about the food she still had on her shelf. Maybe the crying soldier would like a package of cheese and crackers.

But soldiers could get that food any time they wanted. That wouldn't be much of a gift.

"I can't do this anymore," Parvana heard the soldier say, between sobs. "I can't do this. I'd rather be dead!"

Then Parvana knew what to do.

She hopped down from her perch, dug the pen and a piece of paper out from under her mattress.

She would write the crier a note. It might cheer

him up. Or at least it would make him feel less alone.

She put the tip of the pen on the paper. But she couldn't think of what to say.

She started to write, *At least you're not Jane Eyre*. But what if the crying soldier hadn't read the book?

She couldn't write, *It will get better*, because it probably wouldn't. She couldn't write, *Don't worry*, because there were all kinds of good reasons to worry about a lot of things.

It was hard to write a hopeful message because Parvana didn't have any more hope. To have hope would mean that she could see a future that could be brighter than the present.

For a long moment she kept the pen hovering over the paper.

Then she knew the perfect thing to write.

It was a poem she had learned from the book of American poetry. It was by a woman named Dorothy Parker.

Razors pain you;
Rivers are damp;
Acids stain you;
And drugs cause cramp.
Guns aren't lawful;
Nooses give;
Gas smells awful;
You might as well live.

She wrote the poem out, tucked the pen back into its hiding place and folded the paper into a little square. She climbed back up on the cot and table and dropped the poem through a gap in the shutters.

She heard the small sound of surprise from the soldier when the paper landed on him. His crying slowed down as he unfolded the paper, and it eased off as he read the words.

Parvana stayed at the shutters and listened to the soldier blow his nose, get up and brush the dirt off his clothes.

"Thank you, whoever you are," the soldier said. For a second his fingertips touched Parvana's. Then he was gone.

Parvana got down from her perch and paced around the cell. She felt really good. She had reached out to a stranger and had helped him to feel better. She had seen a problem and, for the moment, had fixed it.

That was one of the things she had loved best about the school. She knew where everything was. When students had questions, she had answers. She could help a student who felt stupid realize she was smart, and she could help a scared student feel safe.

Parvana settled back down on the bed and put the blanket around her shoulders again. She started to pick up *Jane Eyre*, but then she had a memory.

Years before, she had worked in Kabul, sitting on a blanket in the market, reading and writing things for people who could not read or write on their own. She had sat beneath a window. The woman who lived behind the window was locked in by her husband, but she dropped little gifts on Parvana's blanket, just to say hello. Before Parvana left Kabul, she planted flowers beneath the window to give the window woman something to enjoy.

I'm the window woman now, Parvana thought.

She smiled.

And then she started to shake.

Her chest felt like it was being squeezed by a wide leather strap. She could not get her breath. She climbed up to the window again, pressed her mouth against the shutters and sucked in as much fresh air as she could.

A question kept floating through her mind.

Who will plant flowers for me?

Maybe it was Miss Brontë's fault, or maybe it was the chocolate in the brownie. Maybe it was the wounded soldier's blood still on her T-shirt or the sweet, smoky scent of the Afghan air. Something cut through the wire Parvana had wrapped around her heart. Something reached what she had tried so hard to hide.

Parvana was too tired to fight it off.

She sank to the floor and drew her knees up to her face.

And cried.

SEVENTEEN

A strange noise pulled Parvana from her sleep.
At first she thought some kind of animal had
come into the room and was whimpering because it
couldn't find its way out.

As she grew more awake, she thought it might be
Ava, scared from a bad dream. But Ava and Maryam
were both sound asleep beside her on the toshak.

Then she realized the noise was coming from her
mother.

Parvana wriggled out from beneath the quilt,
careful not to disturb the younger ones, and knelt in
front of her mother.

Mother was sitting in a corner looking at a photograph of Parvana's father. The photo had been
ripped apart by the Taliban and its pieces scattered
in the wind. Parvana had found most of them on
her journeys around Kabul. A few pieces were missing, but there were enough left to see that it was her
father's face. Even in the scant light of the candle
flame, Parvana could see the strength and kindness
in her father's eyes.

"I'm afraid, Nasrullah," her mother whispered at the photo. "What have I taken on? I'm afraid ..."

Mother talking to photographs was not a good sign.

It used to worry Parvana when it happened in Kabul.

Now it just annoyed her.

She picked up the photo. "I miss him, too, Mama."

"How did he die, Parvana? You were with him. The last time I saw him, he was alive."

"The last time you saw him, he was being arrest-ed." She wanted to say, "And you left him in prison so that your precious Nooria would have a better life." But she didn't say that because 1) for a long time, Nooria did not have a better life and 2) be-cause she wanted to get a few more hours of sleep. She knew from experience that arguments with her mother could last for a long time and lead absolutely nowhere.

She put the photo back on the shelf.

"Can't you sleep?" she asked her mother. "Do you want me to make you some chamomile tea?"

Chamomile was one of the herbs they grew in the school garden. It made a very soothing tea.

"I don't like your tone," Mother said.

"Everything is fine," Parvana said. "Our numbers are down, but we're keeping the school open. The students we still have are learning and doing really well."

"It was wrong to let you be a teacher. Now you think you know everything."

Parvana actually had to put her tongue between her teeth and clamp down hard. Otherwise, she would have said, "You didn't let me be a teacher, you needed me to be a teacher. And I'm a much better teacher than Nooria ever dreamed of being."

She had to bite hard until she was sure the words would stay unsaid.

For a long time, Mother didn't speak. Parvana got tired of sitting in silence and moved to head back to the warmth of her bed.

Then Mother said quietly, "Our students are being harassed in their homes. Their parents are harassed for sending their daughters to us. We're losing students. If our numbers keep going down, the charities that fund us will stop giving us money. We'll have to close the school and we will be back to living in some filthy camp."

Parvana suddenly felt full-body tired, weighed down by her mother's despair.

Then she had an idea.

"The people who hate us can't see through the walls," she said.

Her mother sighed. "Just go back to bed."

"They can't see us, so they think that what we're doing here is bad," Parvana said with growing excitement. "Maybe we should have a sort of school festival. Invite the whole village. Students could prepare the food. Different classes could recite poetry or multiplication tables. Students could give speeches on Afghan history or geography. It could be fun!"

"And, Mama, I could sing!" chirped Maryam from the toshak.

Mother just sighed again. "I wish Nooria was here," she said. "She would know what to do."

Parvana had heard enough. She got up off the floor and left the room. She didn't care that it was still night and she would be cold. Her anger would keep her warm.

Mother was never going to see her as a person with important things to say. Why did she even care anymore?

She stomped around the yard, hitting walls with her fists and kicking at stones. Then she rounded a corner at the back of the school and stopped in her tracks.

There were men carrying boxes into the storage shed. They wore traditional clothes and had the black turbans of the Taliban on their heads and rifles slung over their shoulders. Mr. Fahir was with them.

"Please don't do this," Mr. Fahir said. "We are a school!"

One of the rifle-carrying men shoved Mr. Fahir out of the way.

Parvana dropped back behind the building, her brain and her heart rushing a mile a minute.

Should she run and tell her mother? Should she try

to find some kind of weapon? She had a ridiculous vision of grabbing the thick collection of poetry and bashing the men over the head with it.

Think, she told herself.

She peered around the corner again.

The men were gone.

The shed door was closed.

Moving as quietly as she could, she inched her way over to the shed. She touched the padlock that was back on the door.

She heard the front gate close and a truck engine start up. Sticking to the shadows, she got to the guardhouse just in time to hear one of the men snarl at Mr. Fahir, "You say one word about this to anyone, your whole family dies."

The truck sped off.

Parvana waited a moment, then raised her hand to knock on the guardhouse door.

Then she heard a sound and dropped her hand. She moved in close to be sure.

Mr. Fahir was crying.

She backed away and returned to her bed. She didn't know what else to do.

The next morning, Mother announced at the staff meeting that the school was going to have a festival and invite everyone from the village. Parvana didn't even think about being bitter for not getting credit for the idea. She had much more serious things on her mind. She threw herself into the preparations and stayed away from the storage shed.

Whatever was in there, she didn't want to know.

EIGHTEEN

The festival was just a week away.

"I know it's not much time," Mother said when she announced the plans to the rest of the school during morning assembly, "but you are all well prepared already. Your teachers tell me you are working hard in your studies, and this will give you a chance to show off your talents and knowledge to the whole community."

The girls were enthusiastic. Many of them had tried to explain to their parents what they did all day, but if their parents had never gone to school, it was hard for them to understand.

Now they could show them.

First, villagers would arrive and be formally welcomed by Mother. Then they would visit the classrooms and sit in on a lesson.

Parvana decided her class would do an arithmetic lesson. She had been teaching them about earning and spending money.

She gave them problems to solve: If you have twelve Afghanis, and oranges cost three Afghanis each, how many oranges can you buy? And, if each orange has twelve sections and there are fifteen people in your house, how many sections will each person get?

Or: If it takes twelve spools of thread to embroider a shawl, and each spool costs twenty Afghanis, how much should you charge for the completed shawl to be sure you are making money?

After sitting in the classrooms for a short while, the villagers would be invited to the dining hall for tea and sweets prepared by the students. There they would be entertained by student presentations.

All classes were going to begin by reciting passages from the Holy Qur'an. The little ones were going to sing a song about the animals of Afghanistan. Parvana's class would talk about Afghan geography. The older girls would give speeches about ancient Afghan history. Girls who were keen on singing were going to perform a few Afghan folk songs.

They cleaned the school from top to bottom and decorated it with drawings of flowers, the Afghan flag and traditional Islamic patterns.

The students hand-lettered posters and flyers. Parvana, Asif and Maryam went to the village one day to hand them around. Whenever they could, they taped the festival notices over the threatening notices that were still stuck to the walls.

"Come to our festival," they said to the shopkeepers and to people in the market. "It's free. Come and share the morning with us!"

Asif concentrated on the men. Parvana could see him talking with the butcher, standing close to the headless, upside-down goat. He pointed at the flyer and then up the road to the school. The butcher shook his head and tried to turn away, but Asif wouldn't let him go. He kept talking to the man calmly, until Parvana saw the butcher raise his hands in surrender and say, yes, he would be there.

Parvana smiled and went on with her work.

"Stay with me," she ordered Maryam. Her little sister rarely went to the village, and she kept wandering off.

"I want to explore."

"We're not here to explore. We're here to work."

"I never get to come here," Maryam said.

"You're too young." But as she said those words, Parvana realized that Maryam was almost the age she had been when she first cut off her hair and went to work in the marketplace in Kabul.

"I'll bring you back here after the festival," she promised.

"Mama won't let you. She'll be too afraid."

"She won't be afraid when the festival is over," Parvana said. "People will be so impressed they'll throw flowers in the street for us to walk on."

They put up a few more posters.

Parvana noticed a girl a little younger than herself. She carried a baby in her arms.

"Would you like to come to our festival?" Parvana

asked her, holding out the flyer. "It's at the school outside of town." She pointed the way. "Not a far walk. You can bring the baby. There will be food and lots of things to see."

She held out the flyer, but the girl just looked at her, shaking her head slightly and even backing away a step.

"You are absolutely welcome," Parvana said, thinking the girl might be ashamed of the shabbiness of her clothes. "Come just as you are. I promise you'll be safe and comfortable."

The girl's eyes shifted to the side and she shook her head no again.

At that moment, a man who had been buying fruit at a nearby stall turned around and stood by the girl. He was very tall, very old, and he had an angry look on his face.

He glared down at Parvana and growled, "Get away from her."

Parvana shrank back.

He turned and walked away. The girl with the baby hunched herself over and quickly followed him.

Parvana watched them go, wishing she could snatch the girl away from the old man and stick her in a classroom.

Maryam had disappeared again. Parvana found her at a music stall looking at a girl singing on a small television screen.

"Maryam, let's go."

"It's a singing competition," Maryam said. "Singers from all over Afghanistan get to sing on TV, and people vote on who they like the best. The winner gets a big prize. Oh, Parvana, couldn't I enter? I could win all the money we need!"

"Mother won't let you go to the market by yourself. You think she'll let you go on television?"

She pulled her little sister away from the TV. They met up with Asif and walked back to the school.

Festival day arrived, clear and bright. Parvana was thrilled to see how many people came through the door. Students led their parents in by the hand. Women in burqas walked through the gate on their own and flung their burqas back from their faces once they were in the courtyard. They held onto the flyer as if it was a ticket, in case anyone challenged their right to be there. Even the butcher showed up. Parvana watched Asif welcome him in.

Ava, all dressed up in her school uniform, took the hands of women as they came through the gate and led them to a seat.

Everything went according to plan. The students did what they were supposed to in the classrooms, the guests enjoyed the tea and sweets, and the concert started as scheduled.

And then Maryam took the stage.

She was supposed to sing a traditional folk song.

She was dressed in a tribal dress. Her hair was brushed and looked even longer and thicker than Nooria's.

Why am I the one who got stuck with a head full of string, Parvana thought, as she watched her sister cross to the middle of the open space they were using for a stage.

Maryam took up her position. Then she started to sing.

It took a long moment for Parvana's brain to believe what her ears were hearing.

Maryam was not singing the folk song.

She was singing some pop song she had heard on the radio.

And in English.

It was a love song with a catchy beat, and while she was singing she started to dance.

The dance was simple. Most of it was waving her arms, bouncing her head and jigging her feet in time to the song.

She's pretty good, Parvana thought, listening to her sister's clear, strong voice and seeing the joy on her sister's face. Maybe we *should* put her on television.

She looked at the audience.

The other students were smiling.

Ava, off to the side, had a big grin on her face as she mimicked Maryam's movements.

"Shameful!" a man yelled from the audience. "Shameful!"

The parents sitting around him tried to get him to be quiet. Maryam looked startled for a second, but she kept on performing. The more the man yelled, the louder Maryam sang.

When she finished, the applause from much of the audience was uncertain.

They're not used to enjoying themselves, Parvana thought.

Maryam ran off the stage. Parvana's class was next, and she moved her students quickly into place.

"Afghanistan is a nation that borders Pakistan to the east and Iran to the west. It is made up of many provinces," the first girl said, loud and clear. "Here are the names of the provinces."

The other girls joined in this part, each one saying a province's name in a loud, confident voice. They moved easily from the names of the provinces to the names and length of the rivers, the highest mountains and the major crops. The whole thing was done with speed and joy, and the applause at the end was good.

Parvana's fear eased off, and then the concert came to an end and she was too busy to think about it.

Lunch was served. Mother moved through the crowd answering questions and saying nice things to parents about their children.

Finally, the guests headed out, many carrying little bundles of leftover sweets. Mother closed the gate and leaned against it, sighing with relief.

"I had five people tell me they would send their daughters next week," Mother said. "I think we'll get even more new students than that."

"And Maryam's dance?"

"I'll speak to her. She should not have done it, but your geography class saved it, I think. Well done."

Mother's brief words of praise were so rare that Parvana was shocked into stillness as her mother hurried off to start the clean-up.

Take that, Nooria, she said in her head.

She wandered through the rows of chairs, picking up a fallen napkin, a stray flyer. She was so much in her head, dreaming up other ways she could earn her mother's praise, that she almost walked right by the little girl who was sitting quietly by herself in the third row.

She was not wearing a uniform, so she wasn't a student. Her clothes were shabby but clean, and her hair was brushed and in a neat braid down the middle of her back. Her chador hung across her shoulders like a scarf.

"Waiting for someone?" Parvana asked her.

"Yes."

Parvana looked around. The yard was empty.

"Who are you waiting for? I think everyone has gone."

"The person I'm waiting for hasn't left."

The girl was tiny, but her voice was big, like the voice of a bird that knew it had the right to sing.

"Oh. Well, come with me and we'll look for whoever brought you. They may be wandering around the classrooms. Do you want to come to school here?"

"I am coming to school here."

I'd like her in my class, Parvana thought.

"Come on, then."

She held out her hand.

The girl did not take it.

Parvana noticed that the girl's eyes were focused up and away. She waved her hand a bit. The eyes didn't react.

"Who are you waiting for?" Parvana asked her. "Your parents?"

"Oh, no. They're dead."

"Who brought you?"

"My uncle. But he's gone."

"He left you?"

"I'm waiting for a teacher. Could you get one for me? Tell them Badria is here."

"You're Badria?"

"I sure am."

Parvana decided to take a guess.

"Badria, can you see?"

"Not a thing. Are you a teacher?" Badria asked.

"I am."

"Well, then," Badria said, "don't just stand there. If you're a teacher, get busy. Teach me to read."

Parvana sat down in the chair beside Badria.

She had no idea how to explain this to Mother.

NINETEEN

The cell door banged open.

In shock, Parvana looked up to see several guards, the major and the interpreting woman standing in the doorway, looking at her.

The major approached the bed where she was seated. He picked up *Jane Eyre*, keeping it open to where she was reading, looked at it and returned it to her.

"You got farther than I did," he said in English. The interpreting woman remained silent. "My wife tried to get me to read it for her book club on the base back home."

He stood and looked at her.

"Did you have anything to do with the attack on this base a few days ago?"

Parvana felt sad and heavy.

"It looks like the attack was staged to give you the chance to escape. Some guy on a bicycle blew himself up. Killed two of our people and put a whole lot of others on the injury list. What is so valuable about you that they would send one of their men to his death in order to rescue you?"

Parvana, of course, did not answer.

"It's all starting to come together. We are methodical, and we are going over everything in that school. We have found the remains of munition parts. We are now convinced that materials for building roadside bombs were being stored there. We know you lived there. We have to find out what you know."

He paused, then said, "Enjoy the book."

He started to leave, then turned back.

"Our investigators discovered the body of a woman on the school grounds. It looked like she had been tortured to death. You wouldn't know anything about that, would you? Odd thing was, she was buried with respect, in the Islamic tradition, facing Mecca. We found her under the rose garden."

TWENTY

"Mr. Fahir quit."

It was the day after the festival. Parvana went into Mother's office to report that none of the staff and very few students had shown up for school that morning. It was the last day of class before the weekend. Parvana figured they all just wanted an early start to their time off after working so hard.

"He quit?" Parvana asked. "What did he say?"

"He didn't say anything. He slipped this note under my office door and snuck away in the middle of the night. No notice! And he's got two weeks' pay coming to him!"

Parvana picked up Mr. Fahir's note. The words were clear. *I must quit. I am sorry.*

"We'll manage," she said.

"Maybe one of the teachers has a family member we could hire," Mother said. She stuffed some papers and files in her briefcase. "I'll be back by this evening. Ask Asif to spend the day in the guardhouse. In fact, he'd better move in there until we get a replacement for Mr. Fahir. We don't want people to think we have no man to guard us."

"Mama, take Asif with you."

Her mother would be safer if she wasn't traveling alone.

"And leave you in charge on your own? Goodness knows what you'd get into."

Parvana didn't respond. Ever since Nooria left, she'd been trying not to answer back as much. It seemed immature.

"Then take me," she said. "Leave Asif in charge here."

"You're not getting out of studying. You have a physics exam coming up. Where's my phone?"

Parvana helped her look for it. A car horn sounded.

"There's the taxi," Mother said. "Forget the phone. It's only a meeting of the college planning committee."

She hurried out of the office. Parvana stayed right behind her.

"Are we really going to have a college for women around here?" Parvana asked.

"That's what we're working for," Mother said as they crossed the yard. "We tell our students to study hard and finish high school, but then what? Are they just supposed to stop learning? That's not good enough. We need a college."

Mother unlatched the door in the metal gate. Parvana followed her through it and watched her get into the taxi.

"Keep an eye on Maryam," Mother said from the

back seat. "Don't let her run off to Kabul to be on TV."

Parvana waved as the taxi drove off.

"You're in charge," her mother said. "Look after everyone."

Then Parvana realized that Asif was standing just behind her, waving goodbye, too. Mother could just as easily have been talking to him.

She told him about Mr. Fahir. "Mother wants you to move into the guardhouse until she hires a replacement."

"I'll get some projects to work on in there," Asif said. "Any teachers show up yet?"

"We're on our own."

"Not the first time," Asif said. Then he left to fetch his things.

Parvana went inside the guardhouse. She wanted to find the key to the lock on the storage shed.

The guardhouse was small. It had a table and chair by the window, a narrow mat on the floor and a couple of crude shelves with nothing on them. She went over every inch of the room, even lifting up the mat and looking underneath the shelves.

No key.

She didn't know if she was relieved or disappointed.

Then the school day began and she was too busy to think about it.

To make it easier to keep track of everyone, Parvana had all the students stay in the dining hall, each in their own corners. She sat in the middle, listening to the murmured lessons. She was a little afraid of what might happen if the students realized that she and Asif were the only teachers in the school.

"The teachers are in a meeting," Parvana said whenever she was asked. She nodded vaguely in the direction of Mother's office. "They are discussing the reports they'll be writing for your parents."

So far, it was working. Everyone was doing what they were supposed to.

The standard of behavior was pretty high at the school. The girls had waited so long to get here, and they knew that life without school would be boring and difficult.

Ava wandered from group to group, listening in, not bothering anyone.

Parvana wished she knew what to do with Ava. She tried to keep her busy with little jobs like helping in the kitchen and sweeping the courtyard. And she loved to dig in the garden. It was a better life than she had before, but Parvana thought they could make it better for her still. She just didn't know how.

Badria was doing fine. She had totally refused to say who or where her uncle was.

"He has a new wife and she doesn't want to be bothered with me," she said. "So I am here to stay. And if you keep asking me, I'll just stop talking."

And she did. Whenever the question came up, she clamped her lips together and refused to speak.

"I guess she's staying with us," Mother said.

"I guess she is," Parvana agreed.

To Parvana's surprise, Maryam took Badria under her wing, showing her around the school. They spent the whole afternoon and evening together after the festival, wandering from room to room. Badria learned fast. Most of the time, Parvana forgot she couldn't see.

Maryam was the student most likely to get into mischief, so Parvana had her sister and Badria sit near her. Maryam was supposed to be memorizing a poem. Badria repeated every line she said, so they were both learning it.

It was a relief when the school day ended and the students went home. The weekend was about to start. Parvana was looking forward to a couple of days off — although she never had a day that was completely off. There was always work to do.

"We learned the poem," Maryam said, interrupting Parvana's thoughts. "You want to hear it?"

"Of course," Parvana said, then watched in amazement as the two girls performed the poem as a dance, reciting and moving to the rhythm of the words.

"Wonderful!" Parvana applauded. "How do you know what movements to do?" she asked Badria.

"We plan it out while we are learning the poem. Then I have to trust that Maryam doesn't change them while we're reciting."

"Where's Mama?" Maryam asked. "I want to show her. She'll let me go on TV if it's poetry."

"Mother's not back yet." Parvana realized how late it was. "The meeting must be going well. You might be able to go to college one day, Maryam."

"I'd rather go to Hollywood."

"Could I go to college?" asked Badria.

Parvana was in a hopeful mood.

"Absolutely," she said. Why not? Afghanistan was capable of wonderful things. Sending a blind girl to college could be just another one.

"What would you like to be?" she asked Badria.

"A pilot."

Parvana's jaw dropped. Her brain was still trying to find a reply when Badria and Maryam burst out laughing and skipped off down the hall.

Parvana shook her head. "Save me from little girls," she said. Then she went back to work.

She decided to clean her mother's office. She dusted the shelves. When she swept under the desk, her mother's cell phone came out with the dust.

Parvana pressed buttons here and there. Her mother had promised to show her how to use it after Nooria left, but she never got around to it.

She almost dropped the phone when she heard her mother's voice.

"Hello? Parvana? Anyone there?"

"It's me, Mama! I'm here!" Parvana yelled, then shut up when she realized her mother was continuing to talk.

"Of course you're not there. You are all at lessons.

I don't know what's happening here. There's no meeting and no one seems to know anything about it. I'm borrowing this phone from a shopkeeper. What a big waste of the day. And I'm probably leaving this message to myself."

The phone went silent.

Parvana shook it, not knowing what else to do.

She started going through the desk, looking for information about where her mother had gone — an address, an organization's name, a phone number — anything. She found a government phone book, lesson plans, teacher-training guides and blank writing paper.

But no clues about where her mother was.

"Why didn't I ask more questions?" Parvana cried. "Why didn't I pay more attention to what she was doing?"

The only drawer left to explore was the bottom one. Parvana opened it. It held just one thick file. She put the file on the desk and looked inside.

It was full of letters.

Each letter was a threat.

Parvana counted seventeen of them. All were nasty.

She read as many as she could stand, then closed up the file and put it back where she had found it.

At supper time, Parvana and Asif kept the conversation going around the table, quizzing the younger ones on their lessons and working hard not to look at Mother's empty chair.

For the rest of the evening, Parvana strained her ears for the sound of the returning taxi. She wanted to open the gate and stand in the road, watching for headlights, but she couldn't make the others worry.

Finally, the children were asleep. Parvana left the school grounds and stood in the middle of the narrow dirt road.

She could see tiny lights from faraway lanterns and cook fires. The sky was lit up with a billion stars.

But no car lights and no Mother.

"This is familiar," Asif said from the open window of the guardhouse. "Watching you wait for your mother."

Parvana leaned against the guardhouse wall.

"I was thinking the same thing," she said. "I keep losing her."

"What will we do if …"

"Her meeting is running long, that's all."

"If it's a long meeting, it's probably a good one."

"Yeah. Probably planning a really big college."

"Go to bed," Asif said. "I'll watch for her."

But Parvana couldn't do that. She sat in the dirt with her back against the wall.

She heard Asif sigh and draw back from the window. A moment later he handed her a blanket and sat down beside her, his own blanket shawl around his shoulders.

He started to sing and Parvana joined in — one of the songs they had sung together years before when

they wandered in the wilderness, looking for someone who could look after them. They sang just loud
enough to keep their voices busy and not afraid.

Long after Asif curled up on his side and fell
asleep, Parvana remained awake and watchful as
the constellations traveled across the sky, then faded
into gray.

She could not remember a time when she did not
believe she was on the edge of a disaster. Her life had
gone from battle to battle, and she was never, ever
sure that the future would not be terrifying.

And just when it started to look like things were
getting quiet and back to normal, her mother had to
go to a meeting and not come home on time.

TWENTY-ONE

Morning arrived without Mother.

"You said she'd be back by now," Maryam whined when Parvana and Asif walked into the dining hall after their night on the cold ground.

Parvana looked at the four children lined up on the bench looking angry and scared. Even Badria, who could not see, and Ava, who loved Parvana with her whole heart, were joining in the group glare.

Parvana controlled her face. As hard as this situation was, it would be harder if everyone got upset.

"Why are you all just sitting there?" she asked. "Asif and I are cold. And we're hungry. We want a fire in that wood stove, hot tea in our mugs and breakfast on that table. Now! Move!"

She clapped her hands to get them busy. She held Ava back a moment to give her a hug. She wasn't sure how many words Ava understood, and she didn't want the little girl to think she was mad at her. Ava gave Parvana one of her bright smiles, then skipped into the kitchen to help the others.

A short while later they all sat down in a warm

dining hall to hot tea, boiled eggs and leftover nan.

"Where's Mama?" Maryam asked, chewing on nan drizzled with honey.

"Don't talk with your mouth full," Parvana told her.

Maryam swallowed. "Did something happen to her?"

"Mama did not come back last night and it's a good thing she didn't," she said, sternly. "Do you not see what a mess this school is in? Dust everywhere, laundry to be done, a filthy kitchen. Today is going to be a cleaning day!"

She barked out work orders and the kids hustled off.

"You sound just like Nooria," Asif teased.

Parvana threw a piece of bread at him. He had the good grace not to throw it back.

In truth, the school was already clean, and by the time the sun was ready to set, Parvana had run out of made-up chores. She declared a study hall, but no one was studying. They sat in silence at their books, straining their ears for the sound of Mother's taxi.

It was a night without wind, so every sound could be clearly heard inside.

"She's home!" Maryam said, but when they all rushed to open the gate, "Mother" turned out to be a small flock of flat-tailed sheep herded by a lone shepherd.

The next time they heard a noise it was a pick-up truck full of melons, on its way to the next village. When Maryam said, the third time, "Someone's coming," Parvana told them to stay in their seats. All this dashing to the door wasn't doing them any good.

Then she heard a vehicle pull up to the gate and honk its horn to be let in. They all jumped up.

But it wasn't Mother. It was the police.

Parvana pushed the younger ones back behind the gate and stayed back there with them. She peered out to watch as Asif greeted the two policemen with a respectful "Salaam alaikum" as they got out of the car.

"Can we help you?" Asif asked.

"This man has reported that his wife is missing," the officer said. "He thinks she may have come here."

"There's no one here but us," Asif said. "We are only young. The head of the school is at a meeting and will be back soon. Perhaps you could return tomorrow."

"She has to be here," came a voice from the back seat. "She's not in the house and there's nowhere else she knows of to go."

Out of the back seat came a very tall, very old man.

Parvana gasped. It was the old man from the market.

"I am sorry to hear about your missing wife," Asif said. "She is not here. I swear to you. I have been keeping watch all day at this gate, and no one has come here."

"She went missing two days ago," the tall man said. "Her name is Kinnah."

"She is not here," Asif repeated firmly.

"Are you going to take the word of a crippled boy?" said the man. "I should have gone to the Taliban. They know how to deal with wives who don't behave."

"That's enough," the officer said. "We can handle this." He turned to Asif. "We need to come in and look."

"Of course," said Asif. "You are welcome."

Asif fumbled with the gate latch, giving Parvana time to get everyone out of the way and into the shadows.

Finally, out of frustration, the old man knocked Asif into the dirt — Parvana heard him fall — and yanked the gate open.

"Tear the place apart!" the old man roared.

The police and the tall old man went from room to room in the school. They moved fast. Asif, on his crutches, had to hustle to keep up. Parvana was afraid of what the old man might do to Asif, so she followed at a little distance. She kept her face covered by her chador so the old man would not recognize her.

"This is your liberation?" the old man said, as they left another empty room. "Where girls are allowed to do as they please? She belongs to me. Her father gave her to me to pay off his debt. If she does not come back to me, I will go to the Taliban and her father will pay me — one way or another."

He turned on Asif again. "Have you hidden her? Has she become your wife now? I will kill you both!"

"No one is here but us," Parvana said, stepping forward. She wanted to take his attention off Asif.

"Who is this? Another one of your girlfriends?"

"She is my sister," Asif said. "Our mother runs this school."

"You should teach her to keep silent. Women with big mouths. This is what Afghanistan has come to." He looked beyond Parvana to the children behind her. In steps he was at Hassan's side and had scooped the little boy into his arms.

Hassan screamed.

"My wife has my child. It's a girl. Either I get my wife and daughter back or I will come back here and take this boy. One boy is easily worth the two of them. One healthy boy, that is," he added, sneering at Asif.

"But your wife is not here!" Asif said, reaching for Hassan. The old man held the little boy too high for Asif to grab him.

"I'm talking to the police," the man said. "I'm letting them know what I will do. And they will be responsible, not me."

He gently put Hassan back on the ground. "One week! Then I will be back for you."

Hassan ran to Asif and buried his face in Asif's remaining leg.

One of the policemen moved the beam of his flashlight across the yard.

"What's in that shed back there?" he asked, shining his flashlight.

"Nothing," Parvana replied. "School supplies. I mean, cleaning supplies. Brooms. Nothing."

The men were already walking toward it.

"Unlock it," they ordered Parvana.

"I don't know where the key is," she said. "Our old chowkidar kept it, but he quit and took the key with him."

"What is his name? Where does he live?"

"I ... I don't know," Parvana said.

One of the police officers took his gun out of its holster.

"Hey!" Asif shouted. Hassan and Maryam screamed.

But the officer didn't shoot Parvana. Instead, he shot off the padlock.

We should all run, Parvana thought, as the men entered the shed, flashlights blazing.

"Nothing but boxes of pencils and notebooks," Parvana heard them say.

In a moment they came out again.

"We will be watching," the police said. "If we find out that you are hiding her, the school will be closed and you will be arrested. Do you understand?"

They got into the police car.

"We will be back," one of the officers said.

Then they drove away.

Parvana grabbed a lantern from the dining room and went out to the shed. At first all she saw were boxes stacked neatly against one wall. She opened one up. Pencils. She put that box on the floor and opened the next one.

Grenades.

"Parvana?"

Asif was calling to her.

"I think we have a problem," she called back out to him.

"I know we do," he replied.

She stuck her head out. "My problem is in here."

"Mine is out here," he said. "And I guarantee mine is bigger."

And then Parvana heard a baby crying.

She held up her lantern. From behind the latrine came the girl Parvana had talked to in the market. Her face bore the signs of a vicious beating. In one hand she held a baby. In the other she held a can of kerosene.

"Let me stay or I'll set us both on fire," the girl said. "I'm not scared to die. I'd rather die than go back to him."

No one moved a muscle. Parvana drew a slow, deep breath.

"What did you find in the shed?" Asif asked.

Parvana shook her head.

The grenades could wait.

She knew what to do with scared girls and babies.

"Hello, Kinnah," she said softly. "My name is Parvana. Of course you can stay with us. This is where you belong. Don't worry. Everything is going to be all right."

She talked quietly until the fear slipped from the girl's face.

As the exhausted girl put down the kerosene and handed over the baby, Parvana wondered again when her mother would return.

TWENTY-TWO

Mother returned in a fast-moving car with squealing brakes and spinning tires that sent dust through the open window of the guardhouse into the eyes of Asif, who was keeping watch.

She returned in the company of men with covered faces and big guns.

She sprang from the car as if from a catapult and landed in the dirt with a thud. Asif watched her roll three times before she came to a stop.

He was too scared to move. He stayed in the shadow of the guardhouse until the car had gone, and he could no longer hear the chug of its motor.

Only then did he hobble out to where Mother's body had come to a stop in the weeds.

He could only stand and look at it and will it to move on its own.

"I heard a car," Parvana said as she stepped through the gate. "Is Mother ..."

Her eyes followed Asif's.

And she, too, was frozen.

Somehow, she made herself move.

She walked over to the body and drew back the cloth that covered her mother's head. She stared at the mess the men had made of her mother's face.

There was a note pinned to her mother's clothes.

This woman ran a school for evil girls.
Now she is dead. Her school will be closed.

TWENTY-THREE

*D*ear Nooria:

Parvana was sitting at her mother's desk. She hadn't slept in a long time.

In front of her was Nooria's most recent letter. Someone in America had offered to pay for her flight home during school vacation, and she had written to ask Mother's opinion.

Dear Nooria:
I am writing this instead of Mother because …

Parvana scratched that out.
She tried again.

Dear Nooria:
Please come home right away. When you get here, I will have some news for you that I would rather not have to tell you.

That didn't seem right, either.

Dear Nooria:
Yesterday, before the sun set, we laid Mother
to rest in the most beautiful place on the
school grounds ...

She scribbled through that as well.

The family photos were all in Mother's office. The taped-up photo of Parvana's father with the pieces missing, the photo of her dead older brother, killed by a land mine a long time ago, the photo of Mother graduating from university with her degree in journalism. There was no photo of Parvana's baby brother, Ali, who died during the time of the Taliban.

All these people from one family, all dead.

I'm not dead, Parvana thought. And then she did the bravest thing she could think of.

Dear Nooria:
Mother asked me to write to you because she
is very busy trying to set up a new college for
women. She says she misses you and is very
proud of you, but to please stay in New York
for your vacation. She also wants to know if
there is any way you can take care of Maryam
if we can find a way to send her to you. She
says Maryam is getting to be even more trou-
ble than me!
Your sister,
Parvana.

She started to fold up the letter. Then she picked up her pen again and added something at the bottom.

P.S. I'm proud of you, too.

She sealed the letter.

When Maryam goes, I'll be all alone, she thought.

Asif chose that moment to hobble into the office on his crutches.

"The police will be back," he said. "And I took a look inside the shed. Did Mr. Fahir do that?"

"I think he was forced to," Parvana said.

Asif sat down across from her. "Do you think those weapons belong to the Taliban?"

Parvana shrugged. Afghanistan had so many armies now — the foreigners, the Taliban, the people who hated both the Taliban and the foreigners, the drug people and the people who had their own private armies just because they could.

"I'm going to bury them," Asif said. "Out beside the latrines. And then maybe it's time to leave. We could leave tonight and get as far away as we can before the sun comes up."

"But where do we go? Do we just start walking? We could end up in worse trouble."

"What about going to the foreign army? We're kids. They might protect us."

Parvana considered that for a moment, then shook her head.

"They might help us and they might not, but I don't think they would even let us get close enough to explain ourselves or ask for anything. And even if they helped us, they might make Kinnah go back to her husband."

"We have to do something."

Parvana looked past Asif out into the hallway at the Wall of Achievement.

She had an idea.

"I'm calling someone more powerful than the police, and more powerful than the army," she said, picking up Mother's cell phone.

"Who's that?" Asif asked.

"I'm calling Mrs. Weera."

TWENTY-FOUR

"It takes us a while," the major said.

They were all back in Parvana's cell. She had finished reading *Jane Eyre* and was fifty pages into reading it a second time. The language was difficult, but the more she read, the easier it got.

The questioning man tossed his *Constant Gardener* book onto the bed beside her.

"A reward for saving that soldier's life," he said. Then he started his speech again.

"It takes us a while. Our communications networks aren't as reliable as they could be. Power cuts on and off. That's war for you. But eventually, we always get to the bottom of things. In this case, the explosives and bomb-making equipment buried on the school grounds. Would you like to tell us what that stuff was doing there?"

Parvana concentrated on the cover of the *Constant Gardener* book and wondered if the man had liked it.

"What were you doing at that school?" he shouted.

Parvana could sense him standing beside her, not moving, his frustration coming off him in waves.

"Fine," he said finally. "I've given you every opportunity to talk. Every chance to tell us who you are and what you are up to. Do you understand that I can have you locked away? Locked away without a trial! And you will stay that way for a very long time."

He moved to the door.

"There really is nothing more I can say. The path you are on is one you chose for yourself."

He was halfway out the door when he came back in.

"One question — and I'm really curious about this. You have obviously been educated. You have been given opportunities that my countrymen and women are all here fighting and dying to give to everyone in your country. With all the things you could have chosen to destroy, why did you blow up your own school?"

Parvana decided, this one and only time, to break her silence.

She turned her head, looked the man straight in the eye and spoke in perfect English.

"I didn't blow up my school," she said. "You did."

TWENTY-FIVE

"Is this the office of Mrs. Weera?"

Parvana shouted into the cell phone. The connection was bad, and the war planes that zoomed over the school didn't help.

"I need to speak to her right now. My name is Parvana. She knows me. I need her help. I'm at the Leila Academy of Hope. My mother has been murdered, all the other adults have run away and the Taliban or someone is coming after us. I'm here with a bunch of little kids and I don't know what to do. I need her help ... well, get her out of her meeting!"

After many phone calls to finally get the number of Mrs. Weera's parliamentary office, Parvana was in no mood to be polite.

She gave the woman her phone number and the school's location, then hung up.

"Adults are always in meetings," she fumed.

Asif stuck his head in the door.

"Did you talk to her?"

"I left a message with someone." Parvana pushed the hair out of her face.

He sat down in the chair across from the desk.

"How are you feeling?"

"Old," Parvana said. "And tired. It feels like this is never going to end."

Three days had passed since they had buried Parvana's mother. Today would have been a school day, but none of the students showed up. Word must have spread.

At least we don't have to pretend everything is all right, Parvana thought.

"We weren't able to keep the school open," she said. "They won."

Asif didn't say anything.

"It was great while it lasted, though, wasn't it?" Parvana said. "We really started to build something here. It was like Green Valley, only a thousand times better. Green Valley got destroyed, too."

"What do you mean, too? This school isn't destroyed."

"It is! Mother said that as long as we were open, we were winning. The gates were closed the last time I looked."

"You are such a fool," Asif said, getting out of the chair. "You are the biggest fool that ever lived." He left the office.

"What do you mean? I am not!" Parvana stood up and went after him.

She found him in the dining hall, leaning against the door frame. She saw what he was looking at.

Asif was right.

She was a fool.

Seated around a table were Maryam, Badria, Ava, Hassan, Kinnah and her baby. All were bent over books. Maryam was quietly reading to Badria and Badria was repeating it, word for word. Little Hassan was showing Ava and Kinnah how to write the letters he knew. They were copying them down on their own sheets of paper. Kinnah's baby, cleaned up and fed, was watching everything intently with her big brown eyes.

Everyone was learning.

The school wasn't closed at all.

TWENTY-SIX

Rung by rung, Parvana climbed the ladder, one hand grasping the handle of a can of paint left over from when the school was constructed. She climbed with great care, planting each foot firmly before moving herself up. The moon gave just enough light for her to be able to see where she was going.

The foreign army had moved their explosions closer and closer to the school. Each day brought more helicopters, more low-flying jets that roared so loud that they hurt Parvana's ears, more shooting from the hills. Several missiles had landed on the hill right behind the school.

The shooting was almost constant. Parvana couldn't tell if someone was shooting at the school or shooting at somebody else and the school was just in the way. At least some of the shooters were either not good shots or they were deliberately trying to scare the children. When Parvana or Maryam went out to the garden for onions, or to the hen-house for eggs, gunfire would land in the dirt near them. Bullets would be shot into the walls behind them.

"Maybe they don't know we're a school," Asif suggested.

Which is when Maryam piped up that they should paint the word SCHOOL on the roof in big English letters, so that the foreigners, if they were the ones shooting, would know it was a school and put their guns away.

When Parvana reached the roof, she had a moment of sheer panic. She couldn't remember how to spell school! Was there an h or not? Probably not. The h would make no sense, but she was sure she had seen one in there.

She started with the s, making it big and wide. She did the c because she knew that came next.

Then she sat. She simply could not remember.

What if one of the shooters is also an English teacher, she thought. What if he sees that she spelled such a simple word wrong and decides that either the school is no good and deserves to be destroyed, or it really is a home for the Taliban and they are just trying to disguise it as a school?

Parvana searched her brain and drew a blank.

Then she heard a whisper.

"S-c-h-o-o-l."

Badria was at the top of the ladder.

"Are you crazy? Get back down!"

"Asif thought you might be having trouble with the spelling," said Badria. "He told me what to say."

"You tell him I can outspell him any day of the

year!" Parvana whispered back. "Now go back inside. And be careful!"

Badria giggled and went back down the ladder.

Two days had passed since she had left a message with Mrs. Weera's office, and Parvana was pretty sure she had wasted her time and the last of the cell phone's power tracking her down.

No help was coming. No one was going to rescue them. They were on their own, and they were running out of time.

They had tallied up their food, and they could last for quite a while on what was in the storeroom. They had a good water supply, thanks to the pump one of the foreign charities had installed, and they had high, thick walls that gave them some protection.

But Parvana knew — they all knew — that it would just take one rocket, one grenade, one bomb, one mean man with a gun, and all the food and water and walls would mean nothing.

And the police could come back at any time.

They would have to leave.

But where would they go?

Parvana had wandered in the wilderness with hungry children before. She wasn't anxious to do it again. But how could they just wait for the return of Kinnah's husband — and whoever he might bring with him? Wandering in the wilderness was better than that.

She concentrated on painting, and finished the job.

The valley was quiet. Perhaps all the shooters had gone to sleep. Parvana felt close to the stars up on the roof, and she decided to sit a moment before she went inside. She needed a bit of time to herself. She needed to think about Mother.

She wished her mother had liked her more. She wished she hadn't given her mother such a hard time. They always seemed to be fighting. They fought when times were good, when they lived in a fancy house and Parvana was in school, before the Taliban. They fought when times were hard, when they lived in one room in Kabul, her mother trapped there by the Taliban while Parvana went out to work. They fought in the refugee camp, as Mother tried to get Parvana to obey her when Parvana had been running her own life quite well for a long time. And they fought in the school, when they were finally living the dream they had worked so hard for.

But I loved her, Parvana thought. Did she love me?

Her mother had taken care of Parvana in the refugee camp, when Parvana was so sad over little Leila's death. And she had praised Parvana when her class performed well at the festival.

Yes, her mother had loved her.

But she hadn't always liked her.

And when Parvana really thought about it, she had to admit that she hadn't really liked her mother, either. Not all the time, anyway. But she had loved her very, very much. And she was going to miss her.

She was so caught up in her thoughts she almost didn't notice that someone — or something — was slowly coming up the road toward the school. In the darkness she couldn't make it out. It sounded like an animal and it sounded like bells.

She lay flat on the roof and watched it come out of the night and stop at the front gate of her school.

It was a peddler. Parvana saw a thin man with a long beard sitting on a wagon. Pans and pots hung below — their rattling had been the bells she had heard. She saw chairs, wheels, lumber and other things piled high on the cart. She saw an old, tired horse snuffle in the dirt.

The peddler got down from the wagon and knocked on the gate.

Parvana scrambled down the ladder and crossed the yard before Asif made it out of the guardhouse.

"It's a strange time of night to be selling things," Parvana whispered.

"Maybe he's lost and needs shelter for the night."

"Maybe it's a trick."

"The Taliban doesn't need to trick us," Asif said. "They can just blow us up. So can the foreigners."

Asif opened the little slot in the gate. Parvana heard the man say he was lost and tired and would pay if they would give water to his horse and let him and his cart spend the night inside the gate, away from bandits.

Asif didn't even look to Parvana for permission. He just opened the gate to let him in.

Tugging on the reins of the horse, the man and his cart came into the yard. He looked shorter on the ground than he had from Parvana's perch on the roof. He busied himself unhooking the cart. Ava brought a pail of water for the horse.

Only when the horse was drinking did the man look at each of the children, going from one to the other.

I should have grabbed a weapon, Parvana thought. She shifted her eyes from side to side, looking for the nearest stick or shovel.

The man finally came and stood before Parvana. He looked squarely at her, straight in the eyes.

They were exactly the same height.

"Well," he said, "it's not exactly the Eiffel Tower, is it?"

Parvana couldn't take it in. She couldn't understand what he was saying.

And then, all of a sudden, she did.

She reached out, grabbed the man's beard, and pulled.

The beard came off.

Underneath it was her old friend, Shauzia.

"Mrs. Weera sent me," Shauzia said. "How can I help?"

TWENTY-SEVEN

There was too much to talk about and no time to do it.

"There is a safe house in a village thirty kilometers away," Shauzia said. "You can stay there for a day or two until I can arrange to get you to the next place. It will take us a while to get you out of the area, but we'll do it, don't worry."

"Who do you mean by 'we'?" Parvana asked.

"Mrs. Weera's helpers." Shauzia grinned. "You ought to know. You worked with her in Kabul."

"But ..." Parvana was struggling to accept what was right in front of her. "You're supposed to be in France!"

"France?" Asif asked. "Is this that girl you're always writing to?" He looked at Shauzia. "I thought she made you up!"

"You write to me?" Shauzia asked.

"Don't pay any attention to Asif. He's just an annoying boy I found in a cave. Why aren't you in France?"

"I only got as far as Pakistan. I was waylaid by

one of Mrs. Weera's little jobs. You remember what that's like."

Parvana did. Mrs. Weera was a never-ending series of little jobs.

"Now I'm part of an organization," Shauzia said. "We rescue girls from bad husbands and bad fathers and get them to shelters or other safe places. Some of the men are high up in the army or police. They would kill us if they found us. And the foreigners would back them up. No one wants a bunch of women messing with their plans." She paused a moment. "I'm sorry about your mother." Then she looked at Maryam. "You got bigger. And is this Ali?"

"This is Hassan," Parvana said. "I found him, too. Ali didn't make it."

"What about your father?"

Parvana shook her head.

"Oh. Too bad. You liked him a lot." Shauzia shifted gears. "I'm going to smuggle you all out of here."

"Smuggle us out?" Maryam asked. "That sounds dangerous."

"Living is dangerous," Shauzia said. "But we're all brave, aren't we?"

Parvana looked at her old friend and tried to find the little girl she remembered in this confident young woman who moved with such speed and strength, as though there was no problem she couldn't fix. Next to her, Parvana felt clumsy and old.

I'm just tired, she thought, as Shauzia told them

how she had rescued a girl in another province who was being beaten by her father and brother.

The end of her story was cut off by the roar of fighter jets zooming low over the valley.

"Rude," Shauzia said, when the noise had subsided. "I can't stand these rude foreigners. It's the middle of the night. Babies are trying to sleep."

A moment later there was the sound of an explosion. Not nearby, but not far away, either.

"Let's use this nonsense to our advantage," Shauzia said. "How soon can you be ready?"

It was just a matter of packing up some food, water and blankets. Then there was only time for a quick prayer at her mother's graveside before they all piled into the cart.

"Everyone under the tarps," Shauzia said. "It will be a squish for a while, but as soon as we get out of this valley and away from whatever eyes are in the hills, then it will be easier."

A short time later, under the buzzing of still more planes, and through the blackness of the pre-dawn sky, the peddler and his horse and wagon moved slowly out of the gate and down the road, away from the village. The pots and pans were tied down. They no longer jingled. The wheels glided over the dirt, and the horse's hooves, wrapped in cloth and padding, made little noise as the animal pulled the wagon through the night.

Parvana was up at the front, covered by a blanket but able to peer out. Behind her, under the false bundles, the other children sat still and silent. The rhythm of the horse's walk lulled the little ones to sleep between the sound of the planes, and they made it out of the valley without being shot.

"You want to take one last look at your school?" Shauzia asked. She turned the wagon around so they could look through the gap in the hills. The sky was lighter now. They were on a slight rise. The word SCHOOL could clearly be seen, painted on the roof in bright white against the black tarpaper.

The children flung back their blankets to take a look.

The scream of a low-flying jet came up the valley behind them.

It seemed to Parvana to happen in slow motion: the plane flying low over the school, the bomb dropping like poop from the plane's belly, the explosion that burst the school wall open like a giant flower.

Shauzia didn't wait for the dust to settle. She just turned the cart back around and they went on their way.

Parvana eased down under the tarp. She took Maryam's hand and put her arm around Ava. She looked at Asif through the dim morning light and couldn't think of anything to say.

The children moved through the day. Night was falling when Shauzia pulled the cart alongside a nondescript door in a nondescript wall.

She got down from the wagon, knocked on the door and said, "Mrs. Weera sent me."

The gate opened and they were let inside.

They all got down from the wagon and crossed a courtyard with gardens and a children's swing. Shauzia led them right into the house.

The women who ran the place greeted her with hugs and smiles. It was a house of warmth and light and the scent of good cooking.

Parvana took the tea that was handed to her and sank down on a toshak. All around her was kindness and calm, with grown women caring for each other and for children. She heard laughter and women talking about arrangements for beds.

Asif leaned his crutches against the wall and lowered himself to the toshak beside Parvana.

"I like your friend," he said.

"I told you she was real."

Shauzia wasn't sitting. She was bouncing around, talking with the women who ran things, helping with the young ones. She seemed bright, cheerful and at home.

All Parvana felt was loss. The loss of her mother, the loss of her job, the loss of her school. Even the loss of her friend, because although Shauzia was right there in the room with her, the Shauzia she had been having conversations with in her head and in her notebook was the Shauzia who was sitting in a field of lavender and planning a trip to the Eiffel Tower.

That Shauzia didn't exist, and now Parvana felt like she had no one to talk to.

Then she sat up so suddenly that she spilled the last of her tea on Asif's leg.

"Hey!"

Parvana went over to Shauzia and pulled her away from the women she was talking to, out into the quiet of the yard.

"I forgot something," she said. "I need to go back."

"What are you talking about?"

"I have to go back."

"Why?"

"I left my father behind."

"Your father?"

"His bag. I left my father's shoulder bag behind. It's all I have of him. I have to go back."

Shauzia grabbed her arm.

"You can't! There's nothing there. They bombed it, remember?"

"The bag might still be there," Parvana said. "I've looked through rubble before and found good things. I found Hassan in the rubble of a bombed-out village." She shook Shauzia off.

"The foreigners destroyed it," Shauzia said. "Maybe they made a mistake or maybe they thought it should be bombed. Either way they'll be swarming all over it. And if the foreigners aren't there, the Taliban will be, or some other stupid army. Whoever is there, they won't like you!"

"I've lived in Afghanistan as long as you have," Parvana told her. "I know how to look after myself."

"Wait and see how you feel in the morning," Shauzia said.

"No. I need to leave now." Parvana knew that if she waited until the morning, she would talk herself out of it. It was a foolish trip, but she had to make it.

Shauzia looked like she wanted to keep talking Parvana out of going. But instead she said, "Give me a minute."

Parvana stood in the yard. She looked in the window. Hassan had climbed into Asif's lap and fallen asleep. Kinnah cradled her baby. Maryam and Badria were doing one of their dances. One of the women was brushing Ava's hair. Everyone was all right.

If anything happened to her, at least she had done her job. Everyone was safe.

Then Shauzia was back with a blanket and a pack full of food.

"It's not hard to find your way back there," she said. She told Parvana how to do it. "Better not to have a written map. The fewer things written down, the better. We don't want any armies showing up here."

She handed Parvana the food.

"I can't go with you," she said. "I have to get the others to the next safe house. Don't talk to anyone. You won't know who you can trust. And if you are captured, by the police or anyone else, say nothing for as long as you can. Not a word. Your silence will help keep you calm. And no matter what you say, they'll jump on it and twist it and make you crazy. Give me a chance to get everyone moved. Better still," she added. "Don't get caught. Do what you need to do and then get back here. Someone will know where I've taken everyone."

Parvana gave her friend one quick hug. Then she started walking. She did not look back through the window and she did not tell anyone goodbye.

She walked all night, hid out among some boulders during the light of the next day, then started walking again.

By dawn after the second night of walking, she arrived back at the school. She knew it had been blown up, but it was still a shock to see it.

No one else was around. She walked right through what had been a wall.

She picked up broken cups and dropped them again, set chairs and broken bits of chalkboard right side up. The remains of a padlock lay not far from where the shed used to be. She moved through the rubble, shuffling it around until she found her father's shoulder bag under the remains of a table.

The shoulder bag was still intact.

She opened it up and took out the old copy of *To Kill a Mockingbird*. It was the last of her father's books. She and Asif and Hassan had tried to eat pages of it when they were wandering alone and hungry.

"I guess we can eat you again if we have to," Parvana said.

She slung the bag across her shoulders and turned to leave.

She stubbed her toe against the broken school sign. All the words were smashed. *Leila's Academy of* were now all trash. The only word still intact was *Hope*. Parvana picked it up, placed it on a high piece of rubble and dusted it off.

She had almost cleared all the dust from the nooks and crannies of the word when the American army trucks rolled up.

The soldiers got out, and Parvana left her school for the very last time.

TWENTY-EIGHT

"Any last words?" the major asked.

They were outside, in the bright sunshine. Parvana had shackles on her ankles, a chain around her waist and handcuffs around her wrists. Two strong soldiers held her on each side.

"You're being transferred to the prison north of Kabul," he said. "I tried to protect you, but you left me no choice. You could have talked to us but you chose not to. I hope whatever you are hiding is really worth it."

Parvana thought of Kinnah, who would no longer be raped by the old man she had been forced to marry. She thought of Ava, who would always now be with people who appreciated her. She thought of Badria, and knew that Shauzia's friends would find a teacher who could see how smart she was. She thought of Maryam, who would find some way to sing whatever she wanted to sing, of Hassan, who would grow up to be kind to the women in his life, and of Asif, who was acting more like a man than all those crazy bombing, shooting, yelling and hitting men that gave everyone such a pain.

And she thought of Shauzia, who would continue to bring the good taste of real freedom to the girls who just wanted a chance to live.

"Yes," she replied, and she smiled. "It's worth it."

She did not want to cry.

And then she heard something else.

It was the sound of a car horn blaring. It came closer and stopped right next to Parvana. She could feel the heat of the motor against the backs of her legs.

"You let her go this instant!"

A loud, bossy woman's voice hit Parvana's eardrums like birdsong.

"Get those guns out of my face. What do you mean, treating a minor Afghan child in her own country this way? Under whose authority do you dare do this? Get those chains off her!"

There in front of Parvana was the beautiful, furious face of Mrs. Weera, Member of Parliament.

"I represent the Parliament of Afghanistan. I have a letter in my hand from the president of the country demanding you release this child into my custody right now, and if you hesitate even a second, if you take the time to blink or breathe before obeying this order, I will have Amnesty International, Human Rights Watch, the United Nations International Children's Fund, the American Civil Liberties Union and every television station in the world come down on you like a ton of bricks!"

The major started to argue, but Mrs. Weera stepped right into his face and kept shouting until he gave the order and Parvana was released.

The grip Mrs. Weera held her with was as strong as any chain. There was no way anyone was taking Parvana away from her.

"Get in the van," she ordered.

Parvana climbed into the government van and Mrs. Weera got into the seat beside her. The door slammed and the car took off.

They passed the garbage bins.

"Stop!" Parvana shouted.

The van stopped. She jumped out and grabbed her father's shoulder bag from the top of the trash heap. She got back in the van and they sped away, off the base and out into the world.

"I can see that getting older hasn't meant you get into less trouble," Mrs. Weera said.

"I didn't tell them anything," Parvana told her.

"Of course you didn't. You're much tougher than they are. How would you like to get out of those army clothes? I think if you look on the seat behind you, under that blanket, you'll find what you need."

Parvana turned around and lifted the blanket. There was Shauzia's laughing face.

"I figured we still had some catching up to do," Shauzia said. "Are you all right?"

"I'm fantastic," Parvana said.

She didn't know how they had found her. And just now, she didn't need to know.

"What now?" Mrs. Weera asked.

"Oh, I'm ready for France," Shauzia said. "I've had enough adventure. How about you, Parvana? Want to go to France? Climb the Eiffel Tower?"

"Yes," Parvana said. "That's exactly what I want to do."

"Let's do it," Shauzia said. "It's time."

Parvana sat back on the seat and looked out the window at the rocks, dust, poverty, wildness and hard-working people of her country. People who only wanted to live and laugh and not hurt too much.

France would be calm, clean and peaceful. She could learn to speak French, walk wherever she wanted and build her own future.

It would be a good life. A life anyone would envy.

She wondered whether it would be enough.

"On the other hand," she said, "maybe we could rescue a few more girls first. After all, we already know how to do that."

"I guess we could save a few more," Shauzia agreed. "France isn't going anywhere."

"There are some brochures that need folding in one of the boxes on the floor back there," Mrs. Weera said. "You won't mind doing a little job while we drive."

Shauzia got out the brochures and handed a stack to Parvana.

"So," Parvana said, "more of the same, then. More hunger, more fear and more work."

"This is Afghanistan," Shauzia said. "What do you want — a happy ending?"

AUTHOR'S NOTE

When I heard about the Taliban takeover of Afghanistan in 1996, and the crimes they perpetrated against women and girls, I decided to get involved. This started me on a journey that resulted in the first three books about Parvana and Shauzia — *The Breadwinner, Parvana's Journey* and *Mud City.*

Since then, readers have wondered what happened to Parvana after she was reunited with her mother and sisters and living in a refugee camp, still writing letters to her friend Shauzia. Parvana and Shauzia are fictional characters, but in my head they are very real people, and I wondered myself how they were managing in an Afghanistan that is still at war after more than three decades.

In late 1979 the Soviet Union invaded the country, but even after they were defeated in 1989, the fighting continued, as various groups fought for control of the country. The Taliban militia, one of the groups that the United States and Pakistan once funded, trained and armed, took control of the capital city of Kabul in 1996. They imposed brutal and restrictive laws on girls and women. Schools for girls were closed down, women were no longer allowed to hold jobs, and strict dress codes were enforced.

The Taliban also harbored al-Qaeda, the terrorists

who were responsible for the September 11th attacks on the United States in 2001. In response, the US led a coalition of nations into a war in Afghanistan. The Taliban was defeated, and by the end of 2005 a new constitution had been approved and a new president and parliament had been elected.

But the fighting continued. The Taliban returned to fight against the Afghan government and the various foreign military forces that remained in the country. Other regional leaders known as war lords splintered into different groups and have continued to fight for power. A lot of money has gone into Afghanistan for the reconstruction effort. Unfortunately, much of this money has gone to the war or into corruption at all levels.

The Afghan people are trying to rebuild their lives and their country against this backdrop. The years of war and repression left Afghanistan lacking many basic things that other countries take for granted. School buildings, books, chalk, pens and trained teachers are still in short supply. Half the children in Afghanistan still have no access to any kind of schooling. Many Afghans still live in informal refugee camps without water, plumbing or electricity.

And the situation remains difficult, especially for women and children. Their daily lives are still threatened by suicide bombings, armed conflict and other forms of violence.

Violence against women in Afghanistan continues because of poverty, the ongoing instability caused by decades of war, and the clinging of many to a system of values that believes women are property and are to be silent and obedient. Although there are laws on the books against forced marriage — and against child marriage — the laws are seldom enforced. Struggles for women's rights continue, with girls' schools being burned and women activists being assassinated.

Today some foreign countries, including the United States, are moving to withdraw their troops from Afghanistan. But the war continues, and it is not clear who might be the winner in the end.

For the Afghan people, life must go on. And individuals like Parvana, Shauzia and Mrs. Weera are working to make life better. They, and the many, many Afghan women, men and children like them, are the ones the world needs to support. We owe it to them.

The Breadwinner

Deborah Ellis

Eleven-year-old Parvana lives in Kabul, Afghanistan's capital city. Her father works from a blanket on the ground in the marketplace, reading letters for people who cannot read or write. One day he is arrested and the family is left without someone who can earn money or even shop for food.

As conditions for the family grow desperate, only one solution emerges. Forbidden to earn money as a girl, Parvana must disguise herself as a boy, and become the breadwinner.

"A great kids' book ... a graphic geopolitical brief that's also a girl-power parable." — *Newsweek*

"... a book ... about the hard times — and the courage — of Afghan children." — *Washington Post*

Hackmatack Award • Middle East Book Award • Rebecca Caudill Young Reader's Award • Sweden's Peter Pan Prize • YALSA PPYA

Paperback • 978-0-88899-416-5 • $9.95 CDN / $8.95 US
EPUB • 978-1-55498-007-9 • $9.95 CDN / $8.95 US

Parvana's Journey

Deborah Ellis

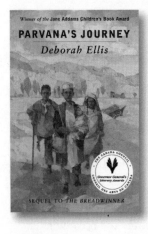

A war is raging in Afghanistan as a coalition of Western forces tries to oust the Taliban by bombing the country. Parvana's father has died, and her mother, sister and brother have gone to a faraway wedding, not knowing what has happened to him. Parvana doesn't know where they are. She just knows she has to find them.

And so, masquerading as a boy, she sets out across the desolate countryside through the war zone that Afghanistan has become.

"Through spare, affecting prose, Ellis ... makes the children's journey both arduous and believable." — *Booklist*

★ "This sequel to *The Breadwinner* easily stands alone... An unforgettable read." — *School Library Journal*, starred review

Jane Addams Children's Book Award • Canadian Library Association Book of the Year for Children Award Honour Book • Governor General's Literary Award Finalist • Ontario Library Association Golden Oak Award • Ruth Schwartz Award • YALSA BBYA

Paperback • 978-0-88899-519-3 • $9.95 CDN / $8.95 US
EPUB • 978-1-55498-030-7 • $9.95 CDN / $8.95 US

Mud City

Deborah Ellis

Parvana's best friend, Shauzia, has fled Afghanistan and now has to survive on her own on the streets of Peshawar, Pakistan. With her dog as her only friend, she must scrounge for food, beg for money and look for a safe place to sleep every night.

But could it be worse than a lifetime spent in a refugee camp? This is a powerful and very human story of a feisty, driven girl who tries to take control of her own life.

★ "A stunning portrait ..." — *Quill & Quire*, starred review

"... a fine, strong addition to Ellis' growing list of novels. Highly recommended." — *Toronto Star*

Hackmatack Award • Lamplighter Award • New York Public Library Books for the Teen Age

Paperback • 978-0-88899-542-1 • $9.95 CDN / $8.95 US
EPUB • 978-1-55498-027-7 • $9.95 CDN / $8.95 US

Kids of Kabul:
Living Bravely Through a Never-ending War
Deborah Ellis

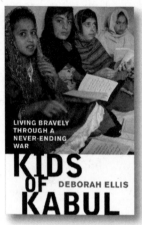

Since its publication in 2000, hundreds of thousands of children all over the world have read and loved *The Breadwinner*, the fictional story of eleven-year-old Parvana living in Kabul under the terror of the Taliban.

But what has happened to Afghanistan's children since the fall of the Taliban in 2001? In 2011, Deborah Ellis went to Kabul to find out. The two dozen or so boys and girls featured in this book range in age from ten to seventeen, and they speak candidly about their lives now. They are still living in a country at war. Yet these kids are weathering their lives with remarkable courage and hope, getting as much education and life experience and fun as they can.

"This nuanced portrayal of adolescence in a struggling nation refrains, refreshingly, from wallowing in tragedy tourism and overwrought handwringing. Necessary." — *Kirkus Reviews*

★ "... compelling and motivating.... A valuable, informative resource." — *School Library Journal*, starred review

Hardcover with jacket • 978-1-55498-181-6 • $15.95
EPUB • 978-1-55498-203-5 • $13.95

ABOUT THE AUTHOR

Deborah Ellis is best known for her Breadwinner series, set in Afghanistan and Pakistan — a series that has been published in twenty-five languages, with more than one million dollars in royalties donated to Canadian Women for Women in Afghanistan and Street Kids International. She has won the Governor General's Award, the Ruth Schwartz Award, the University of California's Middle East Book Award, Sweden's Peter Pan Prize, the Jane Addams Children's Book Award and the Vicky Metcalf Award for a Body of Work. She recently received the Ontario Library Association's President's Award for Exceptional Achievement, and she has been named to the Order of Ontario.

Deborah lives in Simcoe, Ontario.

APR 0 4 2014